SAM

AND THE CURSE OF

THE GREENBACK MONKEYS

BY

DAN WALKER

To my wife and children,

Vanessa, Abigail, Felicity and Peter, who all know the

story well and have encouraged me to write it.

CONTENTS

BEING NORMAL

It was not a normal day. Harry Wright only liked normal days. He had spent his life planning normal days; he led what he believed to be a normal life. He lived in a very nice but normal three-bedroom detached house; he had a normal job as a shipping agent in a normal office working a normal thirty-seven hours a week, earned a normal good sum of money and drove a rather nice but normal car. At the weekend he always wore a pair of chinos, checked shirt, plain-coloured jumper and casual shoes, never trainers. At work he always wore a suit; he didn't like pinstripe so it was normally plain blue or grey with a white shirt and tie. He had six ties and would never wear the same one on consecutive days. His work shoes were either a pair of black or brown brogues, depending on what suit he was wearing. He was of normal build and normal looks. His life was unsurprising, some may even say boring, but it was the life he wanted. He didn't mind not being noticed and was happy to be lost in a crowd. His life was normal.

However, today he was standing on the deck of a sailing boat moored in a berth at Tollesbury Salting in Essex; it was a freezing cold day in early March. He knew the boat well and had previously spent several weeks sailing it, but that was many years ago. He had never enjoyed his time on the boat but was obliged to holiday on board to humour his father who was a keen yachtsman and spent many hours on the boat. It was his father's boat; she was called *Lottie* after his father's grandmother Charlotte Wright and now *Lottie* belonged to Harry, since his father's death earlier on in the year. The boat had been his father's pride and joy. He remembered his father building her over thirty years ago.

Harry stood and looked over *Lottie*. Even he had to admit she was quite an impressive boat. Those who knew about boats would often stand and admire her. She was built along the lines of Sir Francis Chichester's yacht, *Gypsy Moth IV*, in which he became the first person to sail single handed around the world. *Lottie* was just over fourteen metres long from stem to stern and unlike Chichester's boat which was made from cold-moulded Honduras mahogany she was robustly constructed of steel. There were two masts, a tall forward main mast and a smaller mizzen mast which was stepped in the cockpit, making her a ketch-rigged sailing boat. Apart from that, the boat was designed and built to his father's own specification. Notably it included a specially reinforced large forward cabin with a very heavy hatch to the forward deck and watertight door that separated it from the main cabin; both the hatch and door were fitted with multiple locking devices and each had a small window with thick iron bars running vertically from the top to the bottom. Strangely the forward cabin walls were not lined or insulated; they were just left as plain painted steel. When Harry had questioned his father about this, he dismissed the question by saying: it's just not finished yet. The rest of the boat that included the main cabin, sleeping cabin, galley and washroom was exquisitely lined with mahogany woodwork of the highest quality. It had a feel of luxury along with every convenience you would expect from a high-quality cruising yacht – hot and cold running water, heating and a fully equipped galley. According to his father the *Lottie* could safely take you anywhere you wanted to go, anywhere in the world.

Years ago his father would mysteriously disappear for months at a time, much to his mother's annoyance. His parents never spoke about these times and to this day it had remained a mystery as to what he was doing. The only thing that Harry could recall was it seemed that his father was not alone on these adventures. He had met his father's companion on a couple of occasions when he was a young boy over thirty years ago but had no picture of him in his mind, he thought his name might be Sam. His father was not a normal man, he was an adventurer. He wished he had spoken to him more, there were so many questions that remained unanswered, and now both his mother and father were gone he regretted that there were things he may now never know.

So he had become a proud owner of a boat he didn't want and had only caused him to remember parts of his father's life that he wished he knew more about but sadly would never know. The boat itself was in good condition considering its age. His father had maintained her well; even as he got older he would insist on carrying out all the routine maintenance tasks himself and only as a result of his mother's death two years earlier had his father lost interest, not just in the boat, but in Harry's opinion in life itself. Harry reflected on all these things as he stood in the cockpit and wished he had been more interested in his father's life. Harry decided to stay the night onboard, for old times' sake, just one night before he would instruct the local yacht broker to sell the boat for whatever price he could get. That would be an end to it, a final link with this part of his father's life, a farewell and then he could return to the safety and security of his normal life.

Harry was thankful for his father's attention to detail and always keeping the boat in a condition ready to go. It was equipped and stocked with both fuel and long-life food. The below-deck heating was working well. Dusk was just falling when he decided to make one last check on the mooring warps before settling below deck for the night. It was freezing on deck and was going to be a really frosty night. Everything was still and quiet. Harry looked around; he could hear it before he saw it, the soft burbling noise of a boat motoring up the creek coming in with the tide. It was unusual at that time of year to have visitors to the creek so Harry stayed on deck to see who was arriving. Several minutes later the boat came into view, an old wooden gaff-rigged ketch about thirty-two feet long towing a small wooden dinghy. As it came closer Harry could see it was an older yacht and although elderly it looked well cared for.

The white-painted topsides were faded in places which made Harry think if it was his father's it would have been repainted by now. The cabin was made of mahogany with a bright varnished finish. The decks were of laid teak and the rigging was galvanised steel. It was a good well-kept craft, just a little bit worn in places. The sails were neatly furled and although the boat was old she had an air of seaworthiness about her that many owners of newer boats would envy.

As the boat continued to drift slowly on the tide into the salt marshes towards where Harry was standing he could clearly see the name displayed on her hull: *Sandpiper of Tollesbury*. Harry was surprised; he had been in and around Tollesbury Saltings all his life, but he had never seen this boat before.

The salt marshes, or Saltings as they are called in Essex, are desolate places created by the tide depositing silt as it ebbs and flows day after day. They are places which you either love or hate. They are sparsely populated apart from wading birds like the sandpipers, redshanks and moorhens and a mixed-up bunch of old boats safely settled into a variety of mud berths alongside rickety old staging providing a link to the shore. The marshes extended as far as the eye could see, both to the north and south of the creek. As the tide flowed in, small islands of thick grass, saffron and spartina would become cut off from the mainland by water and as the tide ebbed away thick deep mud was exposed, changing the appearance of the salt marsh completely. Most salt marshes can at first glance appear very similar to each other, but this was very different from the others. For as long as anyone could remember this was a very mysterious place, where strange things had happened, things which the local people rarely spoke of to strangers. It was a place rarely visited and a place where children were forbidden to play.

At first sight it looked as though the boat drifting down the creek had no one on board. Then there he was, an elderly-looking man with a well-lined and weather-beaten face, long grey hair and a beard that hadn't been trimmed in some time. He wore an old, thick, cream-coloured woollen jumper, blue canvas trousers and nothing on his feet, even though the evening frost was beginning to bite. He was staring intently at the salt marshes as if looking for something when suddenly his gaze met Harry's. Immediately he turned his boat toward Harry. He seemed pleased and a look of relief spread across his face. As he drew nearer, Harry wondered where he had come from, he looked as if he could have been at sea for months. Why was he here? Without local knowledge it was a difficult creek to navigate, preventing all but the brave from attempting. What Harry didn't know was these were the very last moments his life would ever be normal; within the next twenty-four hours Harry's seemingly boring life would never be normal again!

The stranger's boat drew closer and as it did Harry became concerned as to what he might want. Much to Harry's surprise the stranger seemed to be planning to draw his boat up alongside Harry's. When just three metres away the stranger looked at Harry, smiled and threw his mooring rope, shouting, "Alright, Wrighty, make that fast."

Harry was so taken aback by the use of his name that he completely misjudged the catch and dropped the rope into the water. He hadn't been called Wrighty since he was at school.

"Idiot!" shouted the stranger. "You still can't catch." With a smile he retrieved the rope and threw it again. This time Harry caught the rope and helped the stranger moor up alongside his own boat.

Who is this man? thought Harry. *How does he know my name? Where has he come from?* As Harry was considering these questions, he heard the stranger talking rather loudly. Harry looked around but couldn't see him. The voice was coming from the cabin of the boat now moored alongside his. But who was the newcomer talking to? He decided there must be someone else on the stranger's boat. Harry was trying to decide if he should confront the man or just ignore him and assume the stranger used the term Wrighty with all new people he met, when a head appeared in the companionway of his neighbour's boat, and the stranger looked him straight in the eye and said, "C'mon, Peter, I've just poured the whiskey."

"WHO ARE YOU!" said Harry.

"I know it's been a few years, Pete, but you surely can't have forgotten me that easily," replied the stranger. "It's me, Sam, Sam Shine."

"Two things," said Harry. "One, my name is not Peter and two, I have never, ever…" and as he spoke his voice faded as he recalled a distant memory from more than twenty years ago; he could see himself on board the boat with his father and his father's mysterious friend… Sam.

"Sam," said Harry. "Sam."

"Yes, as I said, SAM, what's the matter with you? Has the salt sizzled your brain?" replied Sam, looking a bit put out.

"Sam, I'm not Peter, I'm Harry, Harry Wright. Peter was my father."

Sam paused for a while, said nothing, just looked at Harry, then he smiled and said, "I remember, haven't you grown? I expect it was a few years or more since we last met."

"A few years," said Harry. "I think I was only six or seven years old, that was over thirty years ago."

"Yeah, maybe," said Sam. "Where's Pete?"

"My father died three months ago."

"What?" said Sam anxiously. "Where? How? Was it here on the Saltings? Tell me, how did he die? I must know."

"It's OK. It was very sad, but he died at home, his home in the village. He was eighty-four years old," said Harry.

"Thank God," murmured Sam as he sank down into his seat. His eyes glazed over and he stared into space. Sam was sure he could see tears forming in Sam's eyes. Silence fell upon the cabin that seemed to last forever, but was probably no more than a minute.

Quietly Sam asked, "Did he speak about me? Did he tell you what we had been doing? Did he tell you our story?"

Harry was quite taken aback. He asked, "What story? What were you doing? He never said anything, it was one of the things Mum hated. He would just mysteriously disappear for weeks at a time then refuse to talk about it."

"Good, good," said Sam. "That's how it needed to be."

"Good!" exclaimed Harry. "It wasn't for us, they were awful times. We never knew what he was doing. We never knew when he was going to go or when he would be back."

"Yes," said Sam, "but you always had plenty of money, you and your mother never went short of anything, mine and your father's business always made sure of that."

"That's not the point," said Harry angrily, "we wanted him at home. What was he doing?"

"I can't tell you, I made a promise to your father that you and your mother would never know."

"Never know what? You must say." Harry was suddenly becoming quite agitated. He didn't like being agitated and he didn't like not knowing the mystery that surrounded his father. He was now face to face with the man who had the answers but wasn't telling.

Harry stood up and stared down on the seated Sam, before deciding that maybe a softer approach would be better. He sat down again and said, "Come on, you really ought to tell me, after all I am his son and he's dead now. What harm can it do to tell?"

"No, I can't tell you," said Sam in a slightly raised voice. "I can't tell. You may be Peter's son, but you really don't want to know, trust me." He stared at Harry and looked much bigger and far more intimidating than he previously had. Harry could clearly see a scar down the left side of Sam's face which only made him look even more threatening close up.

Harry, being unaccustomed to such aggression was starting to feel a little apprehensive about the situation he found himself in. The standoff continued. Then the tension from Sam's face disappeared, he took a deep breath and said, "Let's have a drink. Whiskey?"

Harry's relief was obvious. Sam handed him the glass of whiskey he had poured earlier. As darkness fell, by the light of a single oil lamp the men relaxed and continued to make small talk as they got to know each other a bit better. Finally Harry said again, "Please tell me about my father. What was he doing? Where did he go? I really want to know. I have regretted every day since he died not asking and the thought of never finding out has disturbed me deeply."

Sam thought for a while; Harry could see he was

considering what to do next. Finally he looked at Harry and to Harry's relief he said, "OK, I'll tell you, but be warned, once I've told you, good or bad and there is some bad, like it or not, you will know. And what is told can't be untold." He then looked straight at Harry and said, "Do you really want to know?"

Harry felt the chill in Sam's voice and a sudden fear overcame him, but he did want to know. He sat back in his seat and slowly and clearly he said to Sam, "Yes, tell me. Good or bad, I'm ready, I need to know."

Sam started to tell his story. A story that would have been unbelievable if told by someone else, but a story that was to answer the questions that Harry had had for most of his life, a story that would solve the mystery of the salt marsh, and a story that was destined to change Harry's life forever.

THIS IS THE STORY AS TOLD TO

HARRY WRIGHT ON THAT

NIGHT

Sam Shine was born on the 22nd May 1853. The son of a blacksmith named Jack Shine, who kept a forge at Tollesbury in Essex. His mother, Annie, was the youngest daughter of the local minister. Sam was their only child and by all accounts quite a surprise as the couple had been married for some ten years and had almost come to terms with their childless existence. The blacksmith's shop was very successful and business was booming, providing various iron work to the surrounding farms and while his father worked hard at the forge, Sam's mother ran the local school in her father's church hall. Life was good. Like many youngsters who grow up as the only child, Sam was spoilt, he wanted for nothing. On his twelfth birthday his parents bought him a horse. Not just any horse, they bought him a chestnut Suffolk punch with a white star on her forehead. Suffolk punches were renowned for their strength and gentleness. She was only young, but already showing the potential to be a strong intelligent horse. Sam loved her, he named her Bess and would say that his horse was the best horse in the whole of England. Bess was a fine horse; she was strong and gentle, she could pull a laden wagon well and when needed she could be saddled up and ridden. Bess and Sam were inseparable. Sam was the only child in the village to have their own horse and he was not averse to showing Bess off by riding her at full gallop around the village.

His mother had taught him to read and write and his grandfather had taught him maths. His father taught him how to work the forge. But Sam had no time for any of it. Although bright and able it was neither the forge nor school that was of interest to Sam. What Sam loved best was when his mother would get the atlas out and together they would look at faraway places. His mother would tell him about great explorers and their travels. Sam was inspired by their books and read every one he could get hold of. He wanted adventure, he wanted to escape into a world that excited him, a world that his mother had told him about, a world a million miles away from the village life he was used to.

Sam was not a bad boy, but his behaviour was not always as his parents would have desired. He could be wilful and sometimes a bit cavalier and reckless with no thought as to the consequences of his actions. He was a happy child full of fun. He never wanted to hurt or upset anyone and if he did he was always very apologetic and full of remorse. He was generous and helpful. As a result he was forgiven for most of his minor misdemeanours and was generally very well liked. However, he could not escape his sense of adventure and sometimes this was misguided, notably, the incident that involved the bell in his grandfather's church.

It happened after a night with a small group of friends who he had met behind the local inn. The older boys in the village would often meet there and if they were lucky they could get a flagon of ale from the innkeeper to share in exchange for helping to clear up at the end of the evening. The boys drank the ale and as they did so they discussed what they might do as a dare. Each boy tried to outdo the others with their bravado. One of the lads said he would steal a tankard of ale from the inn, another said they would kiss one of the local girls and a third said he would climb to the top of the old oak tree by the church, a feat that had never previously been done. Sam, not wanting to be outdone by the others suddenly announced that he was going to steal one of the bells from the belfry in his grandfather's church. After all, it had more than one, he thought there were about four or five up there and he was sure no one would miss one. One of the boys said he thought he knew someone who might buy it and as it was made from bronze it could be worth a lot of money. Then a chant went up among the boys. "Do it, do it," they chanted. The ale they had been drinking could have added to their enthusiasm and for Sam he needed little more encouragement. On reflection it was a crazy idea to consider removing a bell from the top of the church tower in the first place. The whole episode was a complete disaster.

The following morning as he stood in front of his mother, father and grandfather he could see that in the cold light of day the funny side may not seem as funny to them as it did to him. After all, it was stealing. In Sam's mind he didn't think it would be too big a problem. As he had tried to explain to his grandfather, there was more than one bell in the tower and the one he tried to take would hardly be missed. He also tried saying that he had been offered a very good price for the bell and that he had some really good plans for how he could use the money to fund an adventure. Every reason he put forward fell upon deaf ears, nobody was listening. Only a lot of long faces, tut-tutting and the sound of his mother quietly sobbing.

Sam resigned himself to the consequences and made some mental notes on how he would carry out the task better next time.

His only mistake was to underestimate the weight of the bell. Sam had carefully placed wooden blocks beneath the bell to take the weight, and then carefully set about tapping out the retaining pin that the bell pivots on. Bit by bit the pin slipped from its socket until with one final blow from the hammer the pin shot out, the bell crashed onto the blocks and then as if in slow motion it leant over to one side, fell from the blocks and burst out through the wooden slats at the top of the bell tower, dropped to the ground, bounced once and rolled through the back door of the vicarage, finally coming to a rest as it slammed into the toilet door. Unfortunately for Sam, his grandmother was in the toilet at the time and was unable to get out until his father and grandfather were able to move the bell. The bell remained in one piece with only a small dent to the side on which it had landed, nevertheless, when it was finally replaced in the belfry, a task which took four men many yards of rope and several pulleys, it never chimed quite in tune again.

Sam spent the next three months maintaining the church and the attached graveyard, cutting the grass and painting the woodwork. It was a long time before he was able to sneak away to meet the other boys behind the inn again.

It was almost a relief to Sam's parents and many of the villagers when one evening Sam came to speak to them with a plan to leave home. He announced he was going to find adventure and he was going to find it at sea. It was his grandfather's idea. Being absolutely fed up with Sam's behaviour, especially after the incident with the bell, he had managed to secure work for Sam on a ship called the *Sea Eagle*. The captain's name was Anderson and he was known to Sam's grandfather through a member of his church who had recently completed some work on the *Sea Eagle*. He had assured Sam's grandfather that Captain Anderson was a very good man who had a reputation of running a very well organised and disciplined crew. Sam's grandfather felt this was just what Sam needed. So it was, on his sixteenth birthday Sam left home to join his ship at Harwich.

The life at sea suited Sam, he loved the sense of adventure. He was eager to learn, fearless and had quickly become skilled at handling the ship in all conditions. He impressed the captain with his enthusiasm and commitment to every task that he took on. The fact that he could read, write and was good with numbers helped make him stand out from the rest of the crew, most of whom had had little education. The captain was keen to develop any member of his crew who he felt worthy and as a result was soon teaching Sam how to navigate and pilot the vessel between the many sandbanks of the Thames estuary and the ports along the north coast of France and further afield to Spain and North Africa. By his twenty-first birthday he had been promoted to first mate, but by his twenty-second birthday he realised that it wasn't going to make him the fortune he aspired to and it wasn't providing the adventure he desired. He had become bored; he wanted an even greater adventure. Captain Anderson was sad to see him leave; in the six years they had been together they had become not just captain and first mate, but also good friends. Sam promised to keep in touch, and his captain assured him that there would always be a place in his crew should he change his mind.

Sam left the *Sea Eagle* early in the morning and set out to walk the thirty miles to Tollesbury and his parents' house. He was hoping that he wouldn't have to walk all the way, often if you were lucky you could hitch a lift part of the way on a farmer's cart or passing tradesman's wagon. He planned to be home before nightfall. He hadn't told his parents he was returning, so after six years and as if no time had passed at all and with little previous contact having been made with his parents apart from the occasional letter, Sam returned home. He had plans.

He made good time and arrived at the outskirts of the village well before dark. As he entered the village of Tollesbury and walked down the once familiar streets towards his family's house and his grandfather's church, a warm sea breeze surrounded him, bringing with it the scent of salt, the salt marsh and the sound of the chirping birds. As he continued he found things very much as they were when he left. There were a couple of new houses on the outskirts of the village and what looked like a recently built baker's shop, apart from that little else had changed. It was clearly a lovely attractive village, even in the fading light of early evening. For his part he was a little broader, his face had become more weathered from his time at sea, his dark hair was long and tied by a bow at the back of his head and he had a scar running from the left eye to just below his left ear, partly covered by his beard. The scar was as a result of a fight he got involved in when he first went to sea.

He was enjoying a night ashore in Hamburg when he noticed a group of three French sailors throwing stones at a dog that they had tied to a post. They seemed to be having great fun making the dog yelp and cheering those who made it yelp the loudest. Sam marched straight over to the dog and released it from the post it was tied to and set it free, at the same time telling the sailors what he thought of their actions in a manner that would be understood if said to you in any language. The response from one of the French sailors, who were obviously very drunk, was to pull a knife from his belt and launch himself towards Sam. Sam was not used to this sort of aggression and was shocked as the blade cut into his face; he fell to the ground only to be surrounded by the other French sailors who proceeded to kick him. If it hadn't been for Captain Anderson arriving at that very moment with two of his crew, Sam would have surely been beaten to death. Captain Anderson along with Billy Bones and John Lyons had turned into the lane just as Sam was knocked to the floor. After a brief scuffle and a lot of shouting, the three drunken Frenchmen quickly made themselves scarce, disappearing at speed down one of the narrow lanes. Sam was forever thankful that on that day the captain had with him Billy Bones – the ship's carpenter and one of the biggest men Sam had ever known, and old John Lyons who for some reason didn't have a specific job on board the *Sea Eagle*, but had always been part of the crew for as long as anyone could remember. As it was, he escaped with bruises and a slashed face and a bond with the captain for saving his life that would last a lifetime. But the grin that stretched across his face was the same as it had always been.

He finally arrived outside his parents' house. He was pleased to see that this too had not changed. It was a little three-bedroom cottage, with a thatched roof and an immaculate front garden full of the most colourful flowers, all courtesy of his mother's hard work of course. He stopped for a moment to admire his childhood home and watched smoke slowly waft out of its crooked chimney. He then took a deep breath but before he entered the house he had somewhere else to go. He had to see Bess. He quietly crept round to the barn at the back of the house where Bess was stabled and there she was. She recognised Sam straight away even though she had not seen him for six years. Sam hugged her, said hello and left. And then as he had always done he entered his parents' house through the back door. His mother was in the kitchen and his father was working at his forge. Sam crept into the kitchen behind his mother; his mother turned, scared by what she saw, not knowing if it was a thief or murderer who had crept into her house. She paused for no more than a second although it seemed longer when she snatched a broom, screamed at the top of her voice and started beating him. It was a full thirty seconds until his father burst into the kitchen waving a blacksmith's hammer above his head ready to strike the intruder down. Simultaneously both parents stopped and stared at the body cowering on the floor. Sam was not the boy who had left home six years earlier, he had now returned home a man, but it was Sam and the smile was still there. Beneath the beard, long hair and scar they recognised their son. Sam's father reached out his hand covered in dirt from his day's work and pulled Sam to his feet, for Sam to be almost knocked back to the floor again by the huge embrace as his mother flung her arms around him. After the initial shock of Sam's return, they sat down and Sam's mother gave him a chunk of freshly baked bread smothered with butter and jam, washed down with a mug of sweet tea. Sam was home. His parents were pleased he had returned; he had left as a boy and returned as a man. And as their only child would now be ready to help his father and take over the business. But he was not home to stay, nothing was further from Sam's mind.

He had a plan. He had saved a small sum of money and with that money he was going to purchase a small four-wheeled wagon that could be harnessed to Bess. Sam was almost as pleased to see Bess still fit and healthy, albeit a bit older, as he was to see his parents and his now elderly grandfather. He had arranged for several large boxes of copper and cloth goods that he had purchased in Morocco in North Africa to be shipped to Harwich; he would load these onto his wagon along with as many pieces of small farm equipment that his father had made in his forge as he could carry. He was going on an adventure – he was going to travel across the country selling his goods to farms and in villages, making a huge profit as he did so. He would travel to all corners of the country, buying and selling as he went. In Sam's mind it was a simple plan that couldn't fail. And once he had made this vast sum of money he would return home and plan the adventure he really wanted to undertake; he was going to the Himalayas, to the highest mountains in the world, Mount Everest. Sam had met a group of sailors on a couple of occasions who had spoken about this range of mountains on the border between India and Nepal, a place where few people had been. In this range of mountains lived the Yeti, a tall bipedal creature covered with long dark hair. Sam had always been fascinated with wildlife but this had really sparked his imagination, he wanted to see one for himself.

So, no more than two weeks after returning from the sea Sam set out with a fully loaded wagon pulled by his horse, Bess, leaving home to search for his fortune. He was glad to be out on the road and out from under the disappointed glare of his parents who had hoped he would stay.

His travels took him as far as St Albans, and to cut a long story short, it was here that his venture came to an abrupt end. He had meandered his way to St Albans, stopping at many towns and villages. It had taken him longer than expected, almost three weeks, but he was at least selling his goods, although he hadn't found much to buy. The problem was he really hadn't been monitoring his expenses very well. Having spent all his working life at sea where all food and lodging was paid for, albeit on board the ship, he grossly underestimated how much it would costs to support himself when he had to pay for everything, including the cost of feeding and stabling Bess. By the time he reached St Albans the money and the goods he had brought with him were almost all gone. He traded the last of the copper bowls that he had imported from Morocco on feed and stabling for Bess and spent his final night in St Albans sleeping alongside Bess in the stables. In the morning he finally came to the realisation that he was miles from home with nothing left in the wagon to sell and no money in his pocket except for two pence. He spent that last two pence on oats for Bess and a pork pie for himself which they both eagerly ate before leaving town.

He stopped just outside St Albans and sat in the shade of a roadside tree to contemplate what to do next, and as he sat there a feeling of complete helplessness overcame him. Could he sell Bess and the wagon? He could sell the wagon and ride Bess home, but he had neither saddle nor enough money to feed the poor horse. Anyway, Bess was his best friend and as things stood at that particular moment in time his only friend. How could he go home, face his parents and explain how his great adventure had been a total failure? How could he get home? He would have to sell the wagon and Bess and that would really leave him to return home with absolutely nothing! He would have to resign himself to taking over the family business and working with his father in the forge. No more adventure, no dreams of finding the Yeti in the Himalayas. He kicked at the dirt beneath his heels in frustration. He then drew his knife from his pocket, unwrapped an apple he had found on the road and cut it in half, giving one half to Bess and eating the other himself.

As Sam sat contemplating his choices, he saw two people in the distance coming his way. One was significantly larger than the other. A man and child, he thought. As they came closer he could see they were both dressed in white trousers and red jackets with red pillbox-style hats. A sort of style of dress he had seen at a circus he once visited with his parents on a rare day out many years ago. Then his eyes fell upon something that he found shocking, the hand of the taller person held a lead that led to a collar round the shorter person's neck, the sort of lead you would use for an animal. Sam hated any sort of cruelty and was incensed to see this treatment of a child. Sam couldn't help himself; he jumped to his feet and shouted, "What on earth do you think you're doing? Free that boy!" And with that he ran at the man and pushed him to the ground. As he did so he glanced at the youngster by the man's side and before he could throw a punch he stopped dead in his tracks. What he saw he had only ever seen on a handful of occasions. The face of the child was completely covered in hair; in fact all exposed parts of his body were covered in hair. Then what followed nearly killed him. The stranger was not a man who was normally pushed about, and as quick as a flash he drew a knife from his belt; it was a Mambele, an African throwing knife with a long curved blade, ivory handle and a rearward protruding spike, and it was a highly effective fighting weapon. He held it in one hand and with the other grabbed Sam by the neck and pinned him to the ground with the blade firmly digging into his throat. "STOP, STOP," Sam growled in a gravelly half-strangled voice. With that, the stranger pushed Sam away and stood up. Sam pushed himself backwards to take stock of the situation. What on earth was he looking at?

"It's a monkey!" shouted the man. "It's a monkey. Have you never seen a monkey before?"

"Yes," said Sam, "but only on a couple of occasions and never in England."

"A monkey," the man repeated. "It's mine, he's from the Gold Coast in West Africa."

As calm returned to the situation Sam could see that in fact it wasn't a child who was being led by the man, it was an animal. He had seen monkeys before and had read about them in books at school. But he had never come face to face with such an animal ever!

"From Africa, you say," enquired Sam.

"Yes, Africa," replied the stranger.

"Well what on earth is it doing here then?" replied Sam.

Standing up and brushing himself down Sam stretched out his hand and apologised. "I'm really sorry," said Sam, "I thought it was a child you had by the lead."

"Well it isn't," said the stranger. "You push me to the ground, upset my monkey and now you're sorry, how dare you? I'll be on my way and you think yourself lucky you still have your life."

With that, the stranger replaced his knife into his belt and set off down the track.

Sam, having been brought up a well-mannered person with a good understanding of right and wrong and seeing the possibility of an opportunity, was keen to make amends.

"Please," said Sam. "Listen, is there any way I can repay you for my foolishness? Let me help you and that monkey, maybe we can help each other."

The stranger stopped and turned towards Sam.

"Tommy, the monkey is called Tommy and my name is Baccary. What have you got? How can you help me?"

Sam again held out his hand. "Sam," he said, "Sam Shine, pleased to meet you." This time Baccary shook it.

Sam thought for a minute and quickly realised that he had very little he could offer.

"Er, I've got a wagon and a horse," said Sam. "Where are you going?"

"The port of Harwich in Essex," replied Baccary.

"Wow, that's nearly seventy miles away," said Sam, thinking out aloud.

"So give us a ride? It's the least you can do."

Sam considered his response. Sure enough he was going that way and Harwich was only just over twenty miles from Tollesbury, but did he really want to spend three or four days travelling with a complete stranger? He had no other option, this could be his only way of getting home complete with Bess and his wagon, so he said, "Just one problem. I don't have any money or food."

Baccary looked at him, sighed and looked to the

sky. This was the first time that Baccary had found himself looking to the sky in disbelief when talking to Sam; it would not be the last.

"You drive the wagon and I'll sort out the rest, I've got a long way to go and Tommy certainly can't walk very fast." And with that, Baccary and Tommy climbed onto the wagon. "C'mon, let's go!" he shouted as he beckoned Sam with his hand.

And so it was agreed, Sam's new companions would ride with Sam as far as Tollesbury, and then they would make their own way to the docks at Harwich where they could board a ship to take them back to mainland Europe where they planned to join with one of the many circuses that travel between the towns and cities of Europe. P. T. Barnum's circus had just arrived in Europe from the United States and it had a reputation of paying well for new acts. Baccary had written to the owner and they had replied saying that if he could get himself and Tommy to Amsterdam they may be able to offer them a job.

The journey from St Albans to Tollesbury took four days. During this time Baccary and Sam shared their stories.

Baccary was a big man; he stood about six feet six inches tall and was not the sort of man you would want to cross. Baccary explained how he was born in a small village on the west coast of Africa by the sea near the city of Accra on the Gold Coast, the name of the village he could no longer remember. Both of his parents had died when he was still young. They had contracted a disease brought into the village by visiting missionaries. It had devastated the village, leaving so few survivors that the village was no longer able to sustain itself and those who had survived quietly left one by one.

By a strange quirk of fate Baccary found himself being cared for by the very group of missionaries whose presence there had led to his parents' death. He and his younger sister Effie were taken to the mission that had been set up in a jungle clearing ten miles inland. It was not a bad life living with the missionaries. They taught him to read and write and they cared for him well, but it was not the life Baccary had wanted. He had come from a family of men who earned their living from the sea and it was to the sea he wanted to go. So one morning he left the mission that had been his home. He just collected a few simple possessions, said goodbye to his sister, promised to return to her and walked out. He was twelve years old and on his own.

His travels took him out of the jungle which had

been his home for so long and into the built-up area of the newly designated capital city Accra. Accra was a busy and bustling port situated on the Atlantic coast. It was a far cry from the quiet village that he was used to and to a young Baccary, quite scary. However, Baccary was big, strong, confident and mature for his age, it wasn't long before he was able to convince a skipper to take him on as a deckhand. His first ship was a small Moroccan sloop that traded up and down the West African coast. He spent ten years working on that ship, he was quick to learn, becoming fluent in speaking French, English and gaining a basic knowledge of several African languages. It was a tough life at sea, but it gave him employment and taught him useful skills and discipline, all of which would prove to be invaluable, especially when he moved onto whaling ships that circled the globe in search of their prey.

In the early days he found it exciting and he could earn good money, especially a strong man like himself, who could handle and use a harpoon with deadly effect. However, the money earned was soon lost through drinking and gambling. It was an occupation that Baccary was finding increasingly distasteful and difficult as the number of whales was decreasing and they were becoming harder to find.

More importantly, the sight of the slaughtered whales started to play on his mind. It was bloody and cruel work. He had never lost the respect for all animals that he had gained from his time in the jungle with the missionaries; they had taught him to respect all life and he was thankful for their influence on his life. Eventually Baccary turned his back on whaling and returned home to Accra.

It was there in a bar that he met a sailor from Brittany who had a small very young monkey as a companion. The sailor had found the monkey who had been separated from his parents on the coast road just outside Accra. Baccary immediately disliked the way the baby monkey was being treated by a man who had a cruel manner and rough ways. When he found that the sailor was prepared to gamble the monkey in a game of poker Baccary did not hesitate in joining the game. He had had years of experience of playing poker on board the whaling ships. Being at sea for years was a good training ground for potential poker players and he was one of the best. The game didn't last long, Baccary placed his bet, and played his cards and left the bar with a little more money and the proud owner of a little monkey. Baccary was pleased with his win. He decided to call the monkey Tommy, after Thomas, one of the kind missionaries he lived with while growing up. It wasn't long before Baccary set about training little Tommy and soon found that people were interested enough to pay money to meet him. He had taught Tommy a few simple tricks, like taking off his hat and pouring drinks from a jug of water. He decided their future lay in Europe where he had heard that there was a developing interest in meeting animals from Africa and there was a good living to be made.

With that in mind Baccary found a job as a deck hand on board a ship heading that way. However, the captain had made it clear when he met Baccary and saw his pet monkey, that there was no way he was going to have a monkey, or any other pet that a crew member fancied bringing, on board. With very little money in his pocket and no other ship leaving for Europe in the foreseeable future Baccary knew what he had to do. He smuggled Tommy on board, burying him under a few simple items of clothing he had in his knapsack. The ship set sail early the following morning. It was quite a struggle, hiding a monkey on board a small two-masted sailing ship. Baccary was unsure of how he was going to feed Tommy; he needed to get fresh fruit and nuts. He had brought some on board with him, but it was not enough to last the whole journey. Eventually he decided to confide his problem with the ship's cook which ended up being a grave mistake. The cook was a small man with long unkept greasy hair and a short temper. It was only out of desperation that Baccary had said anything, but now he felt completely betrayed. The cook's response was to blackmail Baccary with the threat of exposing him to the ship's captain if he did not pay him a large sum of money for Tommy's food and his silence. On a more positive note the cook did have some knowledge of what a monkey liked to eat so a deal was struck.

It was on the fifth day as they neared the coast just thirty miles west of Gibraltar that the worst-case scenario developed. Tommy escaped from the small cupboard in the ship's hold which had been converted into a sort of cage. The monkey, being very clever, was able to mimic Baccary's moves and gestures and had somehow figured out how to undo the lock. Now this wouldn't have been so bad if it had not been for a careless seaman who had left a porthole open. This also wouldn't have been so bad if the porthole had not been directly beneath the place on deck where the ship's captain was standing. As quick as a flash Tommy scrambled through the porthole, up onto the deck and ran through the captain's legs, startling him so much that he fell backwards into the first mate who in turn stumbled and tripped over a stray rope and landed flat on his back. The captain was furious. "What's that monkey doing on my ship?" he demanded.

Instantly the captain lunged out at Tommy, snatched his tail, swung him once around his head and threw him overboard. He then bellowed, "Who brought that creature on board my ship?" He stood with his hands on his hips and as his eyes narrowed he stared at each crew member in turn.

Baccary was on the verge of owning up when suddenly the cook spoke up and pointed. "It was him over there, the African," he said.

The captain drew his sword, and knowing what a violent man the captain could be, Baccary took the only option available to him. He ran to the side of the ship, swung himself up onto the bulwarks, the raised rail that runs above the ship's deck, took one final look behind just in time to see the captain's sword bearing down upon his left shoulder. As he dived off the boat he felt the searing pain shoot though his arm as the blade struck. He surfaced ten metres from the side of the ship and watched as it slipped quickly by, disappearing into the distance, the captain still waving his sword and shouting, "Drown, you scurvy dog, drown!"

Well, you would think that would be the end of the story, and it most likely would have been, for Baccary was in a great deal of pain and was bleeding badly, if it had not been for the great courage and bravery of the ship's cabin boy.

The young lad had discovered Tommy's hiding place late one evening when he was looking for a safe place to keep his own belongings. He was often bullied by the older members of the crew and was in fear that the few possessions he did have would be taken. It was quite a shock for him when he opened the cupboard and discovered Tommy. The noise that the boy and Tommy made immediately woke Baccary who was sleeping nearby; he silenced the boy by putting his hand over his mouth and whispering into his ear that he would cut his throat if he made a sound. Even as he said the words he knew that was something he would never do, he just couldn't think of what else to say. Once he was sure the lad wasn't going to make a sound he let him go. He then introduced the young lad to Tommy and explained the situation they were in, and made the boy promise to keep his secret. He did and became helpful in looking after and caring for Tommy.

The cabin boy had formed quite an attachment to Tommy, and on seeing the monkey being thrown over the side, knew he had to take swift and very dangerous action, for if the captain had seen him he surely would have been in big, big trouble. Secretly, out of the sight of the crew, he took his knife and cut free one of the large empty barrels that would normally be full of water. These were tied to a storage rack fixed to the ship's bulwarks. The barrel splashed into the sea, disappearing below the water before popping up well behind the ship as it sped away into the distance.

Of course Baccary was completely unaware of this and as far as he was concerned he felt lucky just to be alive, even if at that present moment in time his life expectancy seemed to be getting shorter by the minute. His only hope was that another boat would travel along this shipping lane soon. It came as quite a surprise when he spotted Tommy floating towards him riding on top of a water barrel. With all the strength he could muster Baccary swam towards Tommy and dragged the top half of his body up onto the barrel, leaving his legs dangling in the water. With the remains of the rope that was left attached to the barrel after being cut by the cabin boy he tied his arms securely to stop himself from falling off. It must have been then that he passed out because he remembered nothing else until he was woken by the noise of Tommy screeching noisily beside him. His shirt was soaked with blood and his lips had become cracked and dry under the fierce sunlight. As his eyes focussed he looked up and saw the wooden planking of a ship's hull close to where they floated. The next thing he remembered was being dragged up and thrown down onto the deck of a strange ship.

It must have been his lucky day, for the ship was HMS *Java*, a Royal Navy frigate bound for Plymouth. The Royal Navy have a good reputation for looking after shipwrecked sailors found adrift at sea and that is what happened. They immediately moved him to the sick bay where they dressed his wound and fed him and Tommy who was attracting a lot of attention from the crew.

Once in Plymouth he was set ashore with only the clothes he stood up in and of course Tommy for company. With no money and finding himself in a strange town in a country he had never been to before, he set about finding a job. In no time at all and thanks to Tommy being such a novelty he found a job working in a public house just outside the entrance to the naval dockyard. It was there that he and Tommy enjoyed many an evening where he amused the sailors by showing off tricks which Tommy performed faultlessly. These were happy days for them both. But Baccary wanted more, he wanted to see more of the country, he wanted to travel.

After just over a year in Plymouth his chance came when he met the man from the circus. He was persuaded with promises of good money and an easy life to join the travelling circus. At first everything was good, they were given good clothes to wear, plenty of food to eat, but then things changed. The ringmaster started wanting more than to just put Tommy on show, he wanted him to do more tricks, and he wanted him to be more exciting; he wanted him to jump through flaming rings of fire. Baccary went along with it at first and was himself amused by how clever Tommy appeared to be. Then one morning he entered the big top to find Tommy being beaten by the ringmaster with a stick, as the wicked man shouted and cursed poor Tommy, for his failure to complete a trick he had dreamt up the previous evening while drinking with some fellow performers. Baccary flew into a rage.

"How dare you?" he shouted.

He flew at the ringmaster, punching him to the ground. Leaving the ringmaster to nurse his sore head and hangover, he grabbed Tommy, returned to his tent and picked up the few possession he and Tommy had and left. Not a moment too soon for as he crept out of his tent he could hear the ringmaster shouting, "Get me that monkey! Whoever brings me that monkey I will reward with three gold sovereigns."

Baccary ran, carrying Tommy in his arms as he went. They escaped into the nearby woods where they came across a large oak tree. Baccary lifted Tommy up onto one of the lower branches then climbed up into the tree himself; they climbed as high as they could, which for a monkey was easy, for Baccary it was a bit more difficult, and there they hid. They stayed in that tree all night. At the first light of the new day when they were sure no one was out still looking for them they climbed down and set out on their way.

For the second time since arriving in England he found himself on his own with Tommy and just the clothes they were standing up in. Only this time he did have some money in his pocket and a plan. He needed to get away from the circus as quickly as possible, he wanted to get to Harwich where he could board a ship to Holland. He had heard the other performers talking about good opportunities available with some of the circuses that travel around Europe. They had heard that P. T. Barnum's circus had just arrived in Europe from the United States, and they were advertised as the greatest show on Earth. He had previously written to the owner and they had replied to say that if he could meet the circus in Holland, they might be able to offer him and Tommy a job. Baccary decided that now would be as good a time as ever to go and find P. T. Barnum's and see if all they said was true. So with a vague idea of which direction to head, off they went.

Tommy was proving to be remarkably clever, and with lots of encouragement from Baccary he could perform many tricks at a single-word command. He would jump, roll over, catch and throw an apple and for his final trick, when given the appropriate command by Baccary, Tommy would pick up the water, container unscrew the top and pour himself a drink. As the pair travelled across the country Tommy would love to show off his tricks to whoever wanted to watch. Often those watching would gasp at his dexterity and burst into spontaneous applause. Tommy would then remove his hat which he would hold out in front of him while the gathered crowd pressed money into it to show their appreciation of his skills. Finally, Baccary and Tommy reached St Albans where Baccary rented a small room by the clock tower.

In the evening he would walk down to the Fighting

Cock, a local inn by the cathedral. It was a popular place for the locals to meet and drink. He would buy a tankard of ale and sit outside quietly while letting Tommy play with his hat. Then when he had the attention of a small group Tommy would start performing his tricks. Finally as the crowd applauded Tommy would circulate the crowd holding out his hat which the men would place money in as a thank you for his entertaining them. After a few days Baccary and Tommy needed a new audience, and as they always did, they moved on. Early the following morning Baccary dressed Tommy as he always did in his white trousers, red jacket and red pillbox hat, attached his collar and lead, and off they went. It was a pleasant morning, the sun was shining and the birds were singing. Then they met Sam and the story continues.

As the trio travelled together they made several stops at towns along the way. Every time Baccary and Tommy would attract much attention and soon a small crowd would form. Sam was amazed, at not just the showmanship of Baccary and the skill of Tommy, but how quickly at the end of the show people would throw money into Tommy's hat.

The two men chatted to each other constantly as they journeyed, they talked about their time at sea and their desire for adventure, their homes and family.

They had a lot in common. A friendship was developing that would last through many adventures that the two of them could barely have imagined when they first met.

Sam told Baccary how clever he thought Tommy was and how he had never seen such things ever before in his life, and how he wished he had a companion like Tommy.

"That's nothing," said Baccary. He then from the inside breast pocket of his coat produced a piece of paper. It was a map.

"Deep in the jungle of an African country known as the Gold Coast," he explained, "there is rumoured to be a colony of monkeys that are said to be so clever and elusive that men have only seen them on very rare occasions. No one has ever been able to catch one. They say that the monkeys walk like men and that they can communicate with each other using a range of sounds. Their bodies are covered by fur and they have long tails, but if you were to see one you would be stunned by their appearance. They stand upright and proud, but it is their fur you will notice most. Their chest is covered by a fur that shines like silver, but it is their back, their back is covered with a fur that no animal in the animal kingdom has, a fur which when first seen can hardly be believed and when caught in the right light is truly staggering, a fur of emerald green.

"They are so rare, but here, my friend," said Baccary, "I have a map, a map showing exactly where they can be found. It was given to me many years ago by somebody I befriended on a sea journey and now, my friend, I want to share it with you."

Sam could hardly contain his excitement. Was this really a map that would lead him to one of the rarest primates in the world, and was he really one of only a few men that even knew of their existence? His plan for going to the Himalayas and finding the Yeti would have to wait. He had a new adventure waiting for him, he was going to find a Greenback monkey and bring it back to England, he would make a fortune, and Baccary was just the person to help him.

The rest of the journey passed without incident, but Sam couldn't wait to get home; he had things to do and things to organise. He was so absorbed by the thought of his new adventure that he forgot about how he had just failed at the last. It was Baccary that brought him back to earth when he reminded Sam that if it had not been for him, he would still be sitting under a tree near St Albans. Sam simply told him that it would all be fine and he was sure that once he told his parents they would be fully supportive and fully behind him. Baccary, who was a bit more worldly wise, looked to the sky, rolled his eyes and sighed and under his breath muttered, "Things are never that easy." Baccary had instantly liked Sam, he found him to be fun, knowledgeable, intelligent and respectful, but he also knew he was a bit of a spoilt dreamer.

It was a simple plan – go to Africa, catch a Greenback monkey and return – but it was a plan which was to change everything forever, not in a way that anyone in a million years would have ever imagined, but in a way that would lead to trouble, terror and even death.

Sam knew this was his calling, this was the adventure he had been waiting for his whole life.

"Baccary," he said, "we are going to the Gold Coast and we are going to catch a Greenback monkey and bring one back to England."

Baccary expected this to be Sam's reaction once he had shown him the map, but it slowly dawned on him what Sam had said.

"We?" Baccary spun his head round to stare Sam straight in the eyes. "What do you mean 'WE'?"

"Well you can't expect me to make it there alone

and you are the perfect first mate to my captain. We can do this together." Sam said this so casually that Baccary pulled the wagon to a stop.

"But Sam, I can't come with you. I have told you, Tommy and I are off to Europe to join P. T. Barnum's, the greatest show on earth. It could be a really good opportunity for us."

"Baccary," said Sam, "this is an adventure of a lifetime. It is an adventure that we probably have both dreamed of and now it is a real possibility that together we can do this. You can't really leave me to carry out this adventure on my own."

Baccary took a deep breath in and let out a long sigh. He stared at Sam, and as Sam sat there smiling back at him he could see in Sam's face that he was so full of hope; he knew then that deep down inside, Sam was right. There was no way he was going to let Sam go on this adventure alone. He would go with him. But first they had a few things they needed to do.

A New Adventure Begins

Finally the trio arrived at the forge in Tollesbury where Sam was welcomed home with much excitement, not least because of the presence of Baccary and Tommy. The children were amazed, having never seen such an animal before. Tommy kept half the village amused with his tricks. The couple stayed for a month, enjoying the hospitality offered by Sam's parents. Baccary enjoyed helping Sam's dad at the forge and proved to have a natural talent for metalworking which Sam clearly didn't, much to his father's disappointment. Sam spent most of his time with Tommy, showing off his tricks and teaching him new ones. All the time Sam questioned Baccary about Africa and the monkeys he might find there. Finally Sam was able to convince Baccary to come with him and the two men agreed, they would meet up in Accra and track the monkeys together.

Returning to the Gold Coast was something Baccary had been putting off for some time. He had promised his old friend Kojo, the harbour master at Accra, that he would be back months ago. Returning always made him feel uneasy, but he knew it was time to return and meeting up with Sam and helping him was all the excuse he needed. Sam wanted to leave straight away, but both he and Baccary had things to do. Baccary was due in Amsterdam within the month where he hoped to finish the summer season working for P. T. Barnum's circus. He would be finished there at the end of September, he would then need at least two or three months to get to Accra which would mean that he wouldn't be there until the end of the year. That suited Sam, he needed to make some money working for his father and he had equipment and supplies to buy and prepare. So it was decided, they would meet in six months' time, early in the New Year, midwinter in England but summer in the Gold Coast. It would be hot and dry but Baccary had said it would be the best time to hunt and catch one of the mysterious Greenback monkeys.

The following day Baccary and Tommy left. They said their goodbyes to Sam's mother and father, who were both sad to see them go, especially Sam's father who had enjoyed having the extra help. And as he left the house he turned and waved goodbye and said to Sam, "Remember, wait for me, DON'T go into that jungle until I'm with you, it's a dangerous place for those who are not familiar with it." These words would come back to Sam with more meaning later in his adventure.

Sam couldn't wait to get started. But first, he had one thing to do. Tell his parents!

"But Sam, Sam," said his mother, "you promised, you promised that when you returned from your last adventure you would stay and settle down working with Dad."

"I know I did, Mum," replied Sam, "but that was before I had met Baccary, before he had shown me the map that we talked about." He took the copy he had made of the map from his pocket to show them where he was going. "Don't you realise what a brilliant opportunity this could be?"

"No, I'm afraid I don't. Your father needs your help and he needs it now. That place on the map is miles away, how do you know if when you get there, there will be anything there?"

"Mum, you don't understand, I've got to go. I've arranged to meet Baccary. You know I'll never be happy if I stay."

Sam's mother turned to his father who had been sitting silently by the fire smoking his pipe. Before she could say a thing Sam spoke to his father, quietly.

"Dad, you know I must do this, you know, remember those adventure stories you used to read to me when I was growing up and how we used to talk about great explorers? This is my time to do these things and this may be the start of something really exciting and I will always come back to see you and Mum. I've got to do it and when I return, then, then we will see, then if I must, I will settle and work the forge with you happily just as you and Mum wanted and I will be happy in myself. You know if I stay now I will always wonder what would have happened if I had gone."

Sam's father continued to sit quietly, contemplating the flames of the fire for what seemed an eternity. Nobody spoke. Then he turned and looked his wife in the eye. She knew her battle was lost, tears filled her eyes and she left the room.

Sam set to work and for once enjoyed working with his father. With the help of his father together they built a cage onto the back of the wagon using ¾ inch iron bars five feet long, held in place six inches apart by wooden beams placed in a rectangle behind the seat of the wagon. These were in turn held at the top by a similar wooden frame and this was topped with a wooden roof covered in canvas. The rear section of the metal cage had a wooden door fastened with an iron bolt. Canvas tarpaulins were attached to each side of the cage. These were to be kept rolled up and fastened at the top during the day and unrolled to cover the cage at night. Luckily most of the equipment he needed he was able to source from the local farm suppliers. He bought 200 feet of strong rope and a rope net which was normally used to hold down haystacks. He also had a square of canvas which he would use to sleep under. This along with several large metal spikes, a couple of spades, some cooking utensils and one large and one small hammer. Everything was stored on the side of the wagon in wooden storage boxes that Sam's father had made to carry the equipment. Under the seat was another wooden box where food was to be stored and on each side of the cart was attached two small wooden barrels for water to be carried. A small storage compartment was formed in the wagon's floor at the front, under where you would place your feet while driving. This was to carry a small bag of gold coins; money would be useless where he was going. Baccary had advised him to fill the wagon with old tools and equipment that he could trade with the locals when he arrived; he had said that there was always a market for iron tools in Africa. Finally there was, of course, the special compartment which Sam didn't even tell his mother about. In this compartment he placed a Lee Enfield rifle and a Colt revolver complete with a small amount of ammunition, carefully wrapped in waxed paper to ensure they stayed dry. These were expensive items which Sam would normally never consider carrying but his father was insistent and had bought them for Sam to help keep him safe. On wide boards fixed to the top on each side of the cage, written in large red letters was a sign that said, 'Sam Shine, world famous animal trapper and showman'.

Suddenly Harry spoke. "That's your name, was he related to you?"

"Shut up and listen to the story," said Sam. "It will all become clear."

"Was he your grandfather?" asked Harry.

"Just listen," snapped Sam. And he continued.

The year was 1876, Sam was twenty-three years old; he had promised his parents that he would be back before his twenty-fifth birthday. They didn't want him to go. Even when his mother tearfully pleaded with him to stay, he was adamant. He would say, "Don't worry; I'll be back before you know it and I will be rich and famous." There was no changing his mind. He was going and he was going to bring back the monkeys.

Autumn had come and gone and early winter was proving to be wet and cold; it was fast approaching the time to leave. He was looking forward to being at sea again, especially as he hoped it was going to be on board the *Sea Eagle* with his old friend Captain Anderson. He could have left for Africa slightly earlier on another ship that had offered to take him on as crew and had agreed to take Bess and his wagon for a reasonable price. But when he heard that the *Sea Eagle* was heading that way he couldn't wait to contact his old friend and arrange the passage.

He knew that the *Sea Eagle* would be docking in Harwich early in December and had arranged for the harbour master to send him word once it had arrived. On the 10th December he receive the message he had been waiting for, the *Sea Eagle* had arrived. The very next day Sam saddled Bess and rode to Harwich to find the captain. If he wasn't on board his ship Sam knew the captain well enough to know exactly where he would be, and that was where he found him, in a quiet inn just outside town, far enough away so as not to be too easily found but near enough if he was needed. It was his favourite inn and he always stayed there for a couple of nights when in Harwich; it was a good place to have a break ashore after a long sea voyage.

Sam walked into the bar just before midday and spotted the captain almost immediately. It was a good meeting, the men had always enjoyed each other's company and that hadn't changed. They soon set to talking about their time together at sea. The captain reminded Sam of the night he got the scar on his face and if it hadn't been for the captain's timely arrival things may have ended very differently. Eventually Sam told the captain that he wanted to go to the Gold Coast. This was a new route for the *Sea Eagle* since the British Government had taken control of the Gold Coast. Previously it was thought to be too dangerous for any law-abiding trading ships and there was no way the captain would be within five hundred miles of Accra.

At first the captain thought that Sam had wanted to return as a permanent member of the crew and was more than happy to offer him a position as one of the ship's officers. Then Sam explained that it wasn't just him that he needed to take, it was his horse Bess and the specially adapted wagon and he wasn't sure when he would be coming back. The captain wanted to know more – Sam told him; he told him about Baccary, the map, the monkeys, and what he was going to do once he found them. When Sam had finished telling the captain about the adventure he planned the captain smiled, nodded his head and said, "OK." He agreed to take Bess, the cart and Sam, but Sam would have to work and he offered him a position on the crew. The bad news was that the *Sea Eagle* needed some rigging replaced and wouldn't be ready to leave until the New Year, which was later than Sam wanted; he wanted to leave as soon as possible but he had no choice other than to wait. The voyage would take about two months with several stops along the way. At least he got to spend Christmas with his family, which pleased his mother.

Early January the wagon and Bess were finally loaded onto the *Sea Eagle* and the mooring warps were cast off. Snow was lying on the deck and the weather was bitterly cold as the ship slipped out into the North Sea with a freshening breeze from the north-east filling her sails. Sam seemed oblivious to the cold, the excitement he was feeling inside had numbed his feelings on the outside and he couldn't wait to set foot in Africa. Every spare moment he had he studied the map he had copied from Baccary all those months earlier, making sure that nothing was missed and that he understood exactly where he was going. The map was very vague with little detail, but it did show a path and several key landmarks. These included a deserted village with a dried-up well at its centre, a row of six African mahogany trees which led to an area of dense forest with a clearing near its south-eastern edge. The forest was where the monkeys lived and the clearing was the best place to catch them. Finding this place would be a problem for him but he had confidence that Baccary would know exactly how to get there.

Good speed was maintained and progress was good. Even the Bay of Biscay, which is notorious among sailors for its severe storms and giant waves that have seen many a well-found ship flounder, was peaceful, which considering the time of year was a blessing, it was far too cold to be comfortable in poor weather. Often he would disappear below deck and check the wagon, ensuring everything was carefully stored and secure and that Bess was calm, well fed and her stable cleaned.

Things were going well and soon the weather became brighter and warmer the further south they travelled. They stopped at Lisbon and finally Madeira before heading on to the Gold Coast. The north-west coast of Africa was slipping by one hundred miles to port. Maybe things were going too well and it was inevitable that things would at some stage get worse, and so it happened. The sun had risen brightly, the wind had died away, leaving the sea flat, calm and glassy when the shout went out, "Whales on the starboard bow." If ever there was a sight guaranteed to get the men on deck it was whales. They were a common sight at that time of year as humpback whales migrated to their summer breeding grounds off the West African coast. The men would marvel at the majestic way these giants of the oceans would glide through the seas, blowing plumes of spray through the blowholes on the top of their heads like an unstoppable train.

The crew watched, but this wasn't the same as they had seen before; their movement was more erratic, not quite so elegant. The two biggest whales were clearly leading the pod and it was them that would on occasions slow, turn and look at the ship. They then broke away from the rest of the pod and started to slowly circle the ship. The situation started to take on a more menacing feel. Any whisper of wind that there had been had died away completely and the ship sat rolling in the swell. The crew looked on as the two whales continued to circle the ship. Slowly at first they swam alongside, gently bumping the hull as they passed before circling round to start again. Over and over again, each time the thump against the side of the hull would become progressively harder, causing the whole ship to shudder at the impact. Sam had never in all his years at sea seen this sort of behaviour before, but he had heard the stories. Stories of whales battering the side of ships until the timbers splintered and the ships sank were rare but not unknown. The ship's crew were stunned into silence as the whales continued to ram the side of the vessel with increasing force. As Sam watched the whales turn to strike again he remembered a story Baccary had told him, of a similar thing happening to him. He had said it was one of the most frightening experiences of his life. Baccary had said it was only when one of the old sailors had told them to make a noise as loud as they possibly could that the whales finally gave up and disappeared into the depths of the ocean.

"Quickly, make a noise!" shouted Sam. "As loud as you can, now."

Sam started stamping the deck as hard as he could; he took a belaying pin from the rack and started to thump the side of the ship as hard as he could. He was soon joined by several other members of the crew who had recognised they had little else they could do. The ship's bosun joined in with a mallet in each hand which he hammered on the side of the hull, the chef came on deck smashing two saucepans together like a pair of cymbals. Other members of the crew joined in by ringing the ship's bell, drumming the deck with belaying pins or if nothing else was available simply stamping their feet along the side of the deck. Finally Captain Anderson fetched from his cabin a large double-barrelled shotgun which he kept in case of an emergency. He fired into the sea, aiming to the side of the whales. Even at this desperate time his respect for all life meant he was unwilling to harm the creatures. He discharged both barrels then reloaded and fired again. Four times he repeated this action until finally the two whales majestically slipped beneath the surface of the sea leaving only a trail of blood and pieces of splintered wood behind. The whales were gone but the ship was sinking, the damage had been done, and several planks below the waterline had been broken by the force of the whales smashing into the hull.

The ship's carpenter and his team worked through the night under the light of oil lamps to stem the flow of water. As for the rest of the crew, every member had the task of manning the bilge pumps, pumping as hard as they could for one hour at a time or until they could pump no more before the next man would take over. This they did continuously for thirty-six hours while they slowly made their way towards landfall. They were looking for a sandy bay where they would be able to run the ship up onto the beach. Then as the tide ebbed away they would be able to see the damage to the hull and effect a temporary repair. It was a desolate piece of coastline with very few features other than sand dunes and palm trees. Captain Anderson identified a potential spot on the chart he had of the West African coast. However, details on the chart were very minimal. It showed a bay but very little other information, no details about the sea bed or the beach. They would have no idea if there were rocks or any other unknown hazards on this deserted piece of coast. The crew had become very apprehensive especially when one of the old salts reminded everyone that the area that they were sailing towards was known as the skeleton coast.

"It didn't get known by that name for nothing," he moaned.

Captain Anderson gathered the senior members of the crew together. They had no choice, he told them. There was no way they would be able to stay afloat until they reached port, the men were already exhausted and the safety of Accra, the nearest port, was still at least forty-eight hours away. They would have to risk the unknown bay.

Luck was with them and the bay looked to be the perfect place to run the ship up onto the beach. As long as the weather remained settled they would be alright. The ship was anchored about one hundred yards offshore and one of the ship's longboats was lowered into the water. The *Sea Eagle* carried two longboats on her deck, they were basically rowing boats that were used to get ashore if the ship had to anchor out in deep water, they also could be used for towing the ship if needed and finally if the situation needed they could be used as a life boat. Many a sailor had owed their lives to a longboat when disaster had struck and their ship had sunk. The captain instructed Sam to take three men and check the area out before running the ship up onto the beach. It was a fine spot; the sandy beach sloped gently into deep clear water, there were no signs of any dangerous rock outcrops. Sam gave the signal for the ship to be run up the beach.

Once the ship was hard on the beach and the tide had receded to leave the *Sea Eagle* high and dry, the men had eight hours before the tide returned. Bess was unloaded using the donkey net and ropes. It didn't look elegant but it got her ashore and she was able to stretch her legs running up and down the beach. The repair went well; the men worked day and night between tides. They were able to make a good temporary repair using supplies that were normally carried on board. The biggest problem was replacing and reinforcing some of the broken timbers. For this they needed to remove some timbers from one of the lower deck areas and reuse them for the repair. After three days and two nights they were confident enough in the repair to refloat the ship. The ship's two longboats were launched and long ropes attached, one end on the ship and the other to the longboats. Four men manned the oars on each boat. As the tide rose and the water flowed under the hull, slowly the ship began to float. The men in the longboat took up their oars and began to row. Slowly the tow rope tightened and even more slowly the ship began to slip back into the sea.

"ROW! ROW, MEN!" shouted the captain.

The few crew that remained onboard the ship started shouting, "Yes, yes we're moving! Come on, boys! Row, row!"

Finally they were afloat and in deep water. The longboats were brought back on board and the sails set. The mood on board had lightened and as is common on all well-crewed sailing ships the crew burst into song.

Two days later, the Jamestown lighthouse which guides the way into Accra was spotted dead ahead, less than twelve miles away. Five hours later they were safely in port and unloading. Sam couldn't wait to get started. But where was Baccary?

Unbeknown to Sam, Baccary had arrived earlier that month and had gone to stay with his old friend Kojo who he had known since he was a boy. They were both brought up in the mission together. Kojo had stayed at the mission and completed his education there. He was always one of the cleverest children and as Baccary did not have a particular liking of academic subjects he had relied on his help. In return Kojo valued his friendship and it is very useful when you are the small, clever child to have the biggest boy in school as your best friend. Kojo always had his head in a book and often would seem completely distracted and forgetful, his mind often being elsewhere. Baccary recalled how frustrating he would find this when they were growing up together, but Kojo was bright, intelligent and fun so he was always forgiven. He had done well for himself working in the port at Accra and now had a very important job as harbour master, controlling the flow of shipping into and out of the port. He had a fine office and a team of men working for him. He had also, due to his good living, put on a bit of weight and now he was quite a short, rotund man. Something Baccary had great pleasure in teasing him about. Baccary joked about how posh he seemed now and how surprised he was that Kojo would still speak to him. Kojo dismissed his humour with a wave of his hand. However, Kojo did have some news for Baccary, he had bumped into one of the old missionaries a while ago while visiting friends up the coast and he had asked the missionary about Effie, Baccary's younger sister. Kojo had always had a soft spot for Effie and at one time had hoped to plan his future with her. Alas, their plans had taken them in different directions. The missionary had said that he was still in contact with her. And that she had stayed on at the mission, eventually becoming a teacher there. She had left the mission and married a fine man and gone to work caring for and teaching children at an orphanage somewhere to the north-east of Accra. Unfortunately he couldn't remember exactly where but he was sure that someone at the mission would know.

Baccary immediately decided he would have to go to the mission to try and find out more. He left Kojo with strict instructions to send him word as soon as a young English man with a horse and wagon arrived.

The problem was that the mission was at least four days' trek away for a fit person. Kojo, true to his word did send a message to Baccary as soon as Sam arrived, just. He almost forgot; as normal, his mind was elsewhere and it was only as the messenger was leaving that he suddenly remembered. He had to run down the street after him, and he was not as fit and agile as he used to be. Gasping for breath, he passed the message on to the messenger but his breathlessness made him physically unable to express how urgent it was. The messenger had several other messages to deliver and not recognising any urgency, delivered it last. It was seven days after Sam's arrival that Baccary finally received the message.

The day that Baccary received the message was one of the worst days in his life. He couldn't leave the mission, he didn't want to leave the mission, for the man who had taken him in and cared for him and his sister all those years ago, Thomas, was lying frail in his bed. Baccary needed to be by his bedside in his final days, but more importantly he needed to know what had happened to his sister and this man was the only person who knew. Baccary stayed with him until the end then packed up his bag and said goodbye. Without appearing too rushed and rude, he and Tommy left the mission. He was very late to meet

Sam and he made as much speed as he could, hoping that Sam would be waiting for him in Accra. It was nearly five weeks after Sam arrived in Africa that Baccary finally arrived back in Accra at Kojo's house.

"Where is he? Where's Sam?" asked Baccary.

"He's gone, I couldn't stop him," answered Kojo.

"Didn't you tell him to wait? How could you let him go?" said Baccary.

Kojo explained what had happened.

Sam had arrived in Accra and was impatient to get going. Kojo said he had sent a message to Baccary, but Sam wouldn't wait. All he wanted to do was get going. Within three days of arriving in Accra and being unsure of where Baccary was, Sam made the decision to go into the jungle without him. Kojo being concerned for his safety quickly found a couple of young men to guide him, but at such short notice his choice of guides was very limited.

Sam knew he would never be able to do it alone for he had never set foot into a jungle before and he had heard the stories of strange and deadly creatures that live there. From a more practical point of view, he needed the help to widen the path. The map had only shown the trail as a footpath, a fact that was confirmed by Baccary who also told him that most trails leading into the jungle were only footpaths. Making the path wide enough for Bess and the wagon was going to be hard work. So his first action was to find some locals who would be willing to guide him. He was a little surprised initially when the first two possible guides when shown the map of where he wanted to go refused to take him. Their English was not good but it sounded like they were saying the area was a place locals didn't go. Why they didn't go there Sam couldn't understand, but they weren't going to take him there. They had plenty of ideas for places they would take him to but the clearing in the jungle as shown on the map that Sam had copied from Baccary was not one of them. Sam's view was, he hadn't travelled all that way for nothing and there was absolutely no way he was going home empty handed. He would never return home having failed again. For Sam this adventure was all or nothing and he wasn't going to sit around waiting for Baccary, if necessary he would go on his own.

It was while contemplating how he was going to hack his way through the jungle on his own, that Kojo came to find him. He had promised Baccary that he would keep an eye on Sam until he arrived. He had heard that Sam was looking for local guides but none had agreed to guide him, and that he was preparing to go alone without Baccary. Kojo, realising that this would be a dangerous course of action for someone so unfamiliar with the jungle, had decided to try and persuade him to wait. It didn't take long for him to come to the conclusion and understanding that Sam was not going to wait. Sam was clear; he was leaving in the morning with or without a guide. Reluctantly Kojo found two young men, brothers, who needed the work and who needed the money enough to agree to guide him. The pair were not the "sharpest blades" in the drawer, but they were all he could get at the last minute and they were cheap. He wasn't completely happy with the brothers and worried that they may not have been the most trustworthy but they would be better than nothing and Sam looked like he was a man who could manage them.

Sam and his two guides left early the next morning. Seven days after arriving in Accra, Sam was on his way into the jungle. The brothers worked hard and enthusiastically although applying any thought to what they were doing was in short supply. The saying 'less haste, more speed' was appropriate as far as they were concerned. Sam may not have been familiar with the jungle, but he did know how to navigate, and when it came to using a compass navigating on land was not that different than navigating at sea. On at least two occasions he had to stop the brothers and point out that although he was impressed with their enthusiasm and hard work, blindly hacking their way through the jungle in the wrong direction was not helpful to anyone. The brothers just nodded and said, "Yes boss," and then continued as before. Sam soon recognised he would have to keep a close eye on what they were doing if only to ensure their own safety, let alone his.

THE JUNGLE CLEARING

The wagon was fully loaded with water and food. Sam knew that Baccary's monkey Tommy liked fruit and nuts so he made sure he had a plentiful supply and that, apart from three packs of ship's biscuits that he had been given when he left the *Sea Eagle*, was all he took with him. He had already decided that to keep things simple he would eat the same food as the monkeys. As for the guides, they had to bring their own provisions, supplementing them with whatever they could find on the trail. He had expected the whole adventure to take no longer than twenty-eight days at the most. Ten days to get there, up to ten days to catch the monkeys and eight days to get back. He had calculated that the return would be quicker because they would have cleared the path on the way out.

Just as Baccary had said, the clearing was there

right in front of Sam, just as he had imagined. They had found it easily enough, but it had taken four days longer than they planned, fourteen and not ten as Baccary had estimated. And it had been much harder work than anyone could have imagined. Most of the path was just wide enough to walk, let alone wide enough for a wagon. In many places it was so overgrown the path could barely be detected. Sam and his two guides worked tirelessly to clear the way, conscious all the time that there was constant danger from unknown wild animals and poisonous creatures. Throughout the whole journey, day and night Sam could hear roaring and chattering of animals the likes of which he had never heard before. As the group neared the spot identified on the map things started to change. The whole jungle became quieter, just the noise of the men's machetes clearing the path and the occasional rustle as unseen creatures scurried away. Birdsong faded away until it was just a memory and then they were there, standing together in the centre of a small clearing in absolute silence; not a sound, not a breath of wind, nothing.

The clearing was an eerie place, with little sunshine penetrating the canopy of branches and leaves above. It was smaller than he thought it would be, about ten metres in diameter. It was surrounded by tall trees, and the clearing itself was covered with soft grass. However, what made this the most eerie place he had ever been was the silence. They didn't notice it at first, at first there was just a strange feeling of things not being quite right. The brothers were busy setting the trap, laying out the net, camouflaging it with dead leaves and attaching the net to a nearby sapling that was bent double to act as a spring. The trap would be triggered by pulling on a rope which led to a secret position hidden behind a bush where Sam would wait. It was a miracle that the trap was set at all. Again, the brothers set to with speed and enthusiasm and soon had the trap set only for the younger brother to trip over the trigger rope while his big brother was standing in the middle of the net. It sent him flying into the air and left the older brother dangling in mid-air caught in the net. This was followed by much shouting and yelling. Sam just stood and looked completely exasperated. With the amount of noise they were making any monkey with half a brain wouldn't come within miles of them. Eventually Sam regained some control and the trap was reset. Only once this work was completed and the group sat quietly did they notice again how silent the place was. As they hid behind the bush with the rope ready to trigger the trap, the silence and remoteness of their situation hit them. And they waited and waited.

Sam had planned on the whole adventure taking no more than twenty-eight days. Ten days for the journey out and eight days back now the path had been cleared, five days to catch a monkey and five days just in case they needed more time. They had already taken much more time than planned just to reach the clearing, the jungle being denser than anyone had anticipated. The labour of slashing a path through the undergrowth for the wagon had taken its toll on the men; they were exhausted and all appetite for catching monkeys and the money was quickly slipping away. As the hours turned into days there was this slow realisation that time was running out. If they didn't leave soon they would never get home. By the beginning of the seventh day in the clearing the men were getting anxious. They had been away for twenty-one days already and they knew the trip back was going to be arduous.

"We gotta go, boss, we gotta go," they kept saying.

"One more day, just one more day," Sam would reply.

After the tenth day waiting in the clearing and having seen and heard nothing the men were having no more. They were running very low on food and they were going. They gave Sam the ultimatum, come with us or we will leave you behind. The men started to pack their belongings and slowly move towards the wagon. Straight away Sam realised what they were up to.

In a flash Sam leapt up onto the wagon and drew the Colt revolver from its holster; since he had arrived in Africa he had kept it secured to his waist by a wide, thick leather belt. He pointed the gun directly at the men.

"You go!" he shouted. "You go, you scurvy dogs, but I'll shoot the first one of you who tries to take Bess and the wagon."

The men, armed with only their machetes stood staring for a moment. Sam knew there was no going back. If he were to die it would be there right there in the jungle, he had reached journey's end. The men must have recognised this for the standoff between them lasted no longer than seconds, then the men grabbed some supplies and disappeared. The quietness descended once more. Sam was alone. He waited… and waited. He had no other option, he was going to bring a monkey home or die trying.

Then it happened, three days after the guides had left the camp, twenty-seven days since leaving Accra, just as the sun was setting Sam heard a noise, a snapping of twigs perhaps. It was the first noise he had heard for days. His first thought was that it was the men coming back to steal what was left of the food and the horse. He drew his revolver and cocked it ready to fire.

Slowly into the clearing not more than fifteen metres in front of him it appeared, a monkey, a single monkey. Not quite like the ones he had previously seen. It stood on two legs, about five feet tall covered mostly in brown fur apart from a large white patch on his chest and what appeared in the dim light to be green fur down the whole length of his back from his shoulders to his long tail.

Sam placed his gun carefully down on the ground and prepared to spring the trap. Then from his left there entered another monkey, similar to the first only slightly smaller. This was quickly followed by two very much smaller monkeys that appeared to tumble into the clearing, rolling and chattering as they came. Then there they stood, all four of them. A family of monkeys, what appeared to be the father, mother and two children. One of the children was obviously very young.

Sam trembled; this had to be done right, one

chance and one chance only. Slowly he picked up the rope to trigger the trap. With one firm tug the trap was sprung. Whoosh, up it sprang and to Sam's relief all four monkeys were snared in one go. Now how do you get four monkeys hanging from a tree caught in a net into a 10ft by 6ft cage on the back of a wagon single handed? Not through the door, that's for sure. Sam puzzled for a minute. Then quickly climbed onto the wagon and removed the sixteen screws holding down the roof of the cage and removed it. He then pushed the wagon to under where the monkeys were hanging and with one slash of his knife the net complete with the four monkeys crashed onto the floor of the cage. Up until that moment the monkeys had been almost stunned into silence but now they howled and screamed an ear-piercing scream that threatened to deafen anyone who stood too close. Before releasing the captured monkeys from their net Sam made sure the roof was securely replaced.

Sam had planned on the journey back to the port of Accra being much easier. After all, they had already cleared a pathway through the jungle on the way out. However, they had been away for twenty-seven days and had only brought provisions for twenty-eight. It was going to be a difficult journey. Worst of all, the jungle had done what jungles do and had started to grow, reclaiming the path. What was left of the food Sam carefully rationed, giving priority to the monkeys. He knew he was going to be hungry by the time he got back to Accra, but no one starves to death in eight days. They might get very thirsty if they had no water but he was sure he could find additional water on the way back.

The first five days were uneventful, hard work but uneventful, but the lack of food started to take effect and he was feeling very weak. The priority was to feed the monkeys. All of the fresh fruit had been eaten and although he was able to find some in the jungle it was few and far between. He still had a small supply of nuts for the time being, but not enough to last to Accra. Four monkeys were eating far more food than he had planned for. Things were certainly bad but not desperate. Yet!

Sam seemed to bond with the monkeys almost instantly. Ever since he had put them into the wagon and given them food they seemed to be content with their lot. They seemed interested and inquisitive as if they were waiting to see what was going to happen. They chattered and played all day. When Sam placed food into the cage they took it gently from him. At times Sam could believe they were actually talking to him. Sam concluded that they were a lovely family group of monkeys; he could not believe his luck. For once things were going well for him. Yes, there was a shortage of food, but the monkeys were the priority and soon they would be back at the port where Sam could get plenty of food, until then Sam would just have to be hungry.

Disaster struck on the seventh day. It came without warning, quietly, quickly and unexpectedly and as quickly as it came it disappeared. Sam only glimpsed it as it slithered away and disappeared into the jungle, but the damage was done. The most deadly of all snakes, a snake whose poison could kill a man in a day or a horse in less than three, sure enough Bess had been bitten. Bess reared up onto her hind legs, letting out the loudest neigh that Sam had ever heard and then she collapsed onto the ground. There was nothing Sam could do; he had no idea what to do as his faithful friend collapsed to the floor. He sat with Bess. Resting her head in his lap, he stroked his fingers through her mane as the poison slowly took hold and slowly the life drained from poor Bess's body.

Alone with four monkeys in a cage on the back of a wagon only days from safety in the middle of the jungle, he may as well as been a thousand miles from safety, there was no way his journey could continue.

That evening Sam lit a fire. It was surprisingly cold at night and Sam was desperate to try and keep Bess warm and the fire helped keep unwanted visitors at bay. He had never really understood how the locals were able to choose the sort of wood to fuel their fires that produced a lot of heat and very little smoke. His always seemed to produce lots of smoke and very little heat.

Later that evening the hyenas came. Sam tried to scare them away but they returned again and again, every time creeping closer and closer to where Bess lay barely clinging to life. It took every ounce of strength that Sam had left and several shots from his revolver aimed over their heads to keep them at bay until the morning.

The jungle woke to the sunlight with a chorus of sounds, some easily recognisable, others more mysterious. The monkeys, who had so far been surprisingly content living in their new caged environment with its constant supply of food, appeared more agitated than normal. It was as if they could sense something was wrong. Sam thought at times they almost looked sympathetic to his plight. As the day wore on and the sun rose in the sky Sam reflected on what had brought him to where he was now. He remembered the day just outside St Albans where he first met Baccary. How they had fought and then how their friendship had developed. He remembered waving farewell to his friend and the final words Baccary had shouted as he turned and disappeared from sight. How long ago was that? It seemed like a lifetime but barely a year had passed.

By late afternoon all was lost, Sam had fed the monkeys with the last of their food. A quick scout round their camp had confirmed that there was nothing that Sam recognised as being edible. He hadn't eaten a thing for days and the last splash of water he had given to Bess that morning. It would only take two or three days to reach Accra from where they were at most. Should he stay or should he go and try to reach safety alone? He could set the monkeys free and set out to save himself. Although feeling very weak there would be a chance he would get to safety. He would need to decide soon.

The hyenas returned again later that evening, laughing and screeching as they circled the camp. Testing Sam, coming closer and closer, becoming braver with every approach. Sam drew and loaded his revolver again. Should he shoot them? The idea was just a fleeting one; Sam wasn't going to shoot an animal, but he did have to use the last of his bullets from both the revolver and the rifle to keep them at bay until the morning. He didn't sleep well, but was surprisingly almost content and happy with his situation. This was the end, it would be what it would be and he would set the monkeys free, but as for himself, he had nothing to live for, he was weak and could barely walk, he would stay where he was, for it was a fine place and that would be that.

The Smoke in the Jungle

Sam's only slight hope now was that the two local guides who deserted him earlier had told the harbour master about his situation and he had arranged for a search party to find him. However, as the men had left him on bad terms with him threatening to shoot them, he felt that that was probably unlikely. They were unlikely to go back and say they had stolen some of his food and left him alone in the jungle. Sam opened his water container hoping for at least a last drop of water to wet his parched lips. Nothing, not a drop. In frustration he threw the container into the undergrowth, kicked out at the dirt beneath his feet and dragged himself upright and shuffled towards the wagon. "There's no point in us all dying here," he said as he approached the Greenbacks. "No point in us all dying."

"SAM, SAM! Is that you?" It was a voice that Sam

half recognised, but couldn't be. He turned and looked in the direction it had come from but was barely able to focus. He thought he saw a small monkey close by, but monkeys don't talk.

"Sam, it's me, Baccary."

"Baccary, Baccary," repeated Sam in an almost delirious state. "It can't be, you're not a monkey." In his dehydrated and total exhausted state Sam was utterly confused.

"I told you to wait for me."

"Did you not hear me? I said see you in Africa. You didn't wait."

Sam didn't hear a thing, he collapsed there on the spot and darkness passed over him as he drifted into unconsciousness.

He could have been unconscious for hours, days or weeks, he had no idea.

He opened his eyes slowly, his vision was blurred. Was it a dream, and what was he seeing? He vaguely remembered something, was it Baccary, was it Baccary he saw last before he lost consciousness? No, it couldn't be, he hadn't seen Bacci for months. Who was it standing over by a fire with his back to him? Then he remembered Bess. Oh, Bess, was it just a dream? The snake and poor Bess dying in his arms. His thoughts turned to his mother and father waiting for him back in England. He had let them down again. They had placed their trust and faith in him and he had let them down again. He closed his eyes and just lay there, thoughtless as if his head was completely empty. Nothing, his life was nothing, his life was gone!

His eyes opened again; this time things were a little clearer. He lifted his head and looked. It was Bacci and he was walking towards him smiling, he could hear his words...

"Sam, Sam," he was saying over and over. "I told you to wait."

Baccary leant down low over Sam and placed a cup of water to his lips. Still Sam hadn't spoken. Baccary cradled Sam's head, holding it to the water and Sam took a drink and murmured the words, "Bacci, my old friend," before again fading into unconsciousness. Baccary did the only thing he could think of at the time. He wasn't going to let Sam lie there any longer, they needed to be on their way. They still had some distance to travel to be out of the jungle and into a more safe and friendly environment. So without further to do Baccary took the bucket and went into the jungle. He knew what he was looking for – water. It's never far away in the jungle, it's just about knowing where to look for it. Within minutes he was back with a bucket full of water filled from a hidden stream that ran under a thick cover of vegetation. Even if Sam had known what to look for he was in such a weakened state he probably would never have found it. Gently Baccary again offered Sam the cup. Sam sipped the water. After several sips Baccary took what water remained in the bucket and poured it over Sam's head.

"Come on, Sam, come on!" shouted Baccary. "You'll not die on me here. We've got business to attend to."

Slowly Sam sat up helped by his friend. He looked around.

"Baccary," he said, "what's happened?"

"You've been out for two days and I thought you were dead. This is not a good place, Sam, and we need to move out now."

"Bad place," Sam replied, somewhat confused.

"Snakes," said Baccary, "and plenty of them. Snakes by day, hyenas at night, we need to get going or they'll kill us all. I thought you and Bess were both goners when I found you."

"Bess, Bess is dead, I was with her when she died," whispered Sam.

"Well who's that over there? You fool." And he pointed to where Bess was grazing on a small patch of grass thirty metres away.

"What? How? I thought she had died." Sam got to his feet and stumbled over to where Bess stood, put his hands around her neck and hugged and kissed her as he had never done before.

"You really know nothing of the ways of the jungle, do you?" said Baccary. "If she had been any lesser of a horse than a Suffolk punch she would certainly be dead by now, but she is as strong as an ox, is Bess."

Baccary had lived with his family and in the mission for the first twelve years of his life in the jungle. There wasn't much he didn't know about surviving life in the wild.

"When I was growing up in the jungle, one of the first things we learnt was how to deal with snake bites, and I will tell you now, laying down with a horse that has been bitten and hugging their head is not one of them. You're a fool, Sam, but you're my friend."

"I may be a fool, but what sort of person comes out into the jungle to find a fool?" They both laughed out loud. They would be friends forever and that was to turn out to be longer than either of them imagined.

Sam had almost forgotten why he was there, until he turned and faced the wagon where there were four Greenback monkeys staring at them both. *What must they be thinking?* thought Sam.

It was a very slow journey back through the jungle to Accra. Bess had recovered well but was still very weak. To relieve the load that Bess had to pull the two men walked alongside the wagon with ropes attached to the wagon tied around their waists. Between Bess, Sam and Baccary they dragged the wagon yard by yard back to Accra. Baccary's little monkey Tommy was of little help, but he did keep then all amused, even the four monkeys in the cage on the wagon were fascinated by him. Other than the pain of pulling a wagon full of monkeys along the jungle trail the journey was mostly uneventful. They passed close by to some villages. On two occasions people came out to see them, but as soon as they saw the Greenbacks they quickly disappeared back into their villages. If it hadn't been for the smoke rising from camp fires they would have thought the villages were deserted, there was little evidence of any other human life.

It wasn't long before they were back in the town where Sam had unloaded Bess and his wagon six weeks earlier. *Was it only six weeks?* thought Sam. So much had happened it had seemed much longer.

The *Sea Eagle* was in dry dock being repaired from the damaged cause by the whales. After some quick inquiries Sam found Captain Anderson in a nearby bar. Sam, Baccary and the captain spent the evening together. Sam told of his adventure in the jungle which the captain listened to in almost disbelief. He couldn't believe that they had actually found the monkeys, caught them and transported them to the port ready to take them back to England. The repairs to the ship were nearing completion and it would be ready to set sail again the following week. Arrangements were made for Bess, the wagon and four monkeys to be taken back to Harwich. A price was agreed and the deal done. The cost was less than he expected, apparently due to the superstition that ships that had been attacked by whales were unlucky. Sam didn't believe they would be unlucky twice.

Baccary was not going to come with them.

Sam had begged Baccary to return to England with him. Every day up until the ship set sail Sam pleaded with him to come. "Get on that ship and go," Baccary said. "I will come and find you when I'm ready."

"Why? Why? I'm not leaving you and Tommy now, not after all that we have been through."

Baccary explained that while he was visiting the mission before Sam had arrived in Africa, he had the news that his sister Effie, who he had not seen for many years, was living in a village twenty miles up the coast and he was determined to find her.

Sam knew he couldn't stop him and he knew he couldn't stay and for the second time in his life as they parted company Sam cried. Not sobbing tears, but with a sadness that brings tears to the eyes that then roll down the face.

The men hugged, not another word was spoken, the men went their own ways in pursuit of their own aims.

Storm in the Bay

The ship was loaded complete with Sam, a fully rested and recovered Bess, four monkeys in a cage and a wagon. Bess, the four monkeys and the wagon were lowered into the hold of the ship. The crew had created a space in the hold where the monkeys were to be kept. Although they were to spend most of the time in the cage on the wagon, there was also a secure area where they could exercise. This was to delight the crew who found the monkeys to be really playful and entertaining. Bess was returned to the stall that she had travelled out in. She was not amused. But there was a good supply of straw, hay and feed. Sam would ensure that he would spend most of his time during the voyage in the hold with the Greenbacks and Bess.

It was very early on a Tuesday morning that they cast off and set sail out into the Atlantic Ocean. The sun was shining and a fair wind was blowing. Good progress was made. The crew were particularly concerned about suffering from another whale attack; a special lookout was kept and the crew were ready to make a noise if needed and Captain Anderson made sure his shotgun was loaded and ready. Sam quickly settled into a daily routine of feeding cleaning and exercise and most importantly training. Every afternoon Sam would sit outside the cage and try to get the monkeys to imitate his actions. He always had a handful of nuts and an audience of off-watch crew members; every afternoon would be a riot of laughter and fun as they watched the animals play. Gradually as the days passed the monkeys became more confident and a mutual trust between Sam and the monkeys started to develop. Especially with the youngest and sweetest little monkey any of the crew had ever seen. He had clearly been the baby of the family when captured by Sam, and Sam had no idea of exactly how old he could be but he guessed at no more than a few months.

It was on about the fifth day at sea that the little one came to Sam while out playing in the enclosed pen. He came up to the enclosure's perimeter fence, right up to where Sam was sitting, put his hand through the fence and very lightly and gently touched

Sam's arm. Sam could hardly dare to breathe; he continued to sit as close as he could to the enclosure and without moving an inch let the baby monkey explore him with his hand. This went on for several days, Sam would sit by the enclosure and the little monkey would come straight over, push his hand through the fence and touch Sam. Eventually with great care, Sam gently pushed his hand through the bars and stroked the back of the little fella's neck. They became comfortable in the presence of each other. It wasn't long before Sam had, with great trepidation, decided that he was going to open the door and enter the enclosure. This was not something he took lightly, he had thought about this moment long and hard for a number of days before the morning when the decision was made.

Early, straight after placing the morning feed for the monkey into the enclosure he stood by the door and gently eased it open. His heart was thumping so hard he was sure it would scare anyone let alone an enclosure full of monkeys. Slowly he took one step, then another; three steps into the enclosure he sat down absolutely still and waited. The monkeys who were busy eating their morning feed turned and looked at him and without batting an eyelid three of them turned back to the feed and carried on eating, however, his new little friend, nervously at first, walked towards Sam and when no more than two paces away jumped up into Sam's arms and climbed onto his shoulders. Sam sat and they played together on the floor. It was not long before Sam felt confident to take his new friend out of the enclosure and out onto the deck. The older two monkeys seemed to trust Sam with their baby. To keep the monkey safe he gently tied a rope around him and carefully led him out onto the deck. He was worried at first that the parent monkeys may be concerned, but the three remaining monkeys seemed happy to chatter and play happily within their cage. The ship's crew loved it, and it became a daily show, Sam with a monkey on his shoulder walking the deck, all the time the bond between the two of them was growing stronger and as it did, so did the tricks and tasks the little monkey would perform. The time passed quickly, the weather stayed fair and they were soon making a routine stop to take on stores and water in the Canary Islands.

The second part of the journey from the Canaries back to Harwich was unfortunately very different. It started well. It was a bit windy and the waves were a bit bigger than on the first part of the journey, but it was as they neared the Bay of Biscay that the change really started. The Bay is notorious with seamen, for in certain conditions it could become one of the wildest places on Earth. As the Atlantic waves roll into the shallow waters of the bay, giant waves are created causing many ships to founder washed up onto the rocky Brittany shores. This year was to be remembered for some of the worst storms ever witnessed and unfortunately unbeknown to Captain Anderson and his crew, they were heading straight into one of the most violent storms of that year. As the waves and wind increased in size and strength the hatches were battened down, the sails furled and the bilge pumps manned as the ship went into storm survival mode.

For five days and nights no progress was made; the ship was battered and beaten as the waves washed over the decks making any movement outside of the cabin impossible. Anyone who dared to step out ran a real risk of being washed overboard and lost. The ship's wheel was manned at all times by at least two helmsmen who had to lash themselves to the ship with strong ropes to keep them secure. The men took turns in shifts lasting no more than an hour as no man had the strength to endure for longer. No food was cooked, the men survived on ship's biscuits, rum and water. For the duration of the storm Sam stayed in his cabin, only moving out to take his turn at the wheel or at the pump. Every time he left the safety of his cabin his life was in grave danger, at any moment a rough wave could sweep the deck and take anything not tied down over the side and in those conditions if you were to be washed into the sea it would almost certainly lead to your death. All the time he fretted about his precious cargo in the hold but he was unable to help. It was as much as he could do to get to the wheel to take his turn. To manage to get down the whole length of the deck, especially to the more exposed areas up forward including the entrance to the hold containing the Greenbacks and Bess, was impossible in those conditions.

On the fifth day the wind and waves although still battering the ship had abated enough for Sam to risk leaving his cabin and attempting to get to the monkeys; he was now very worried, not just for them but for Bess who was stabled in the same ship's hold in the forward part of the boat. Sam was weary from the days and hours spent manning the ship's wheel and the pump during the storm. Making his way along the side deck was an incredibly difficult and strenuous task. He daren't let his grip relax for every few seconds another wave would wash along the deck. At one point a rogue wave washed him off his feet and if it hadn't been for a rack of belaying pins which he was able to get a firm hand hold on, he would have been lost over the side. Inching his way forward along the deck towards the hold seemed to take forever. Soaked by rain and waves he finally reached the door and steps down to the hold to be met by the ship's bosun. On board most ships there is a ship's bosun, he is the person whose main duties revolve around the deck areas of the ship, supervising the deck crew and ensuring everything on deck is well maintained and secure. The bosun had also become concerned about the welfare of the animals. His cabin was nearest to the hold in the forecastle of the ship, and he had struggled from his cabin from the opposite direction, arriving moments before Sam at the door to the hold. He took hold of Sam's arm and helped him through the door; Sam was thankful for the help. The bosun followed Sam down the ladder.

It was dark down below with the hatches battened closed and the only light was coming from two small skylights set into the roof. The bosun lit two oil lamps which immediately lit up the area. Sam went straight to Bess; she was clearly pleased to see him and Sam her. He was relieved that she was well and after giving her a long hug quickly refreshed her water bucket and basket of hay. He then turned to the monkeys.

Almost immediately he could sense something was wrong – it was silent, not a noise, not a whisper. Sam turned and looked at the bosun, he was standing motionless just in front of the monkeys' cage staring at the floor. Sam looked at the floor of the cage and as he did his blood ran cold and he realised that his worst fear had come true, in fact worse than his worst fear had come true. In the centre of the cage stood three monkeys, shoulder to shoulder in a circle, standing absolutely still and in complete silence. Sam couldn't see straight away or it might have been that he did not want to see. There on the floor in the centre of the circle formed by the animals, lying lifeless was the smallest of then all, the baby of the family, the one Sam had taken to his heart, the most affectionate, the sweetest, the best natured… and now lifeless. Sam just stood and stared, hardly able to believe what he was seeing, tears forming in the corners of his eyes. It seemed like he had been standing there for ages, motionless next to the bosun, when suddenly the bosun stepped forwarded opened the cage door, put his hand into the cage and in less time than it took to blink he took hold of the monkey's small lifeless body, pulled it out through the door and before Sam was able to say or do a thing the bosun was up the ladder onto the deck where he threw the body overboard and was back in the hold, saying, "Done, we don't want no dead animal onboard." Sam had not moved. But the three remaining animals did; slowly they turned to look directly at Sam and as they did they raised their arms and pointed at him and let out an ear-piercing scream the likes of which Sam had never heard before and would never hear again. He didn't know it at the time, but he had just been cursed, the curse of the Greenback monkeys. It would be several years before Sam would find out exactly what this meant and how it would affect him for the rest of his life!

Sam collapse to the floor and sobbed; he stayed for the rest of the day. Things would never be the same again!

*

For the remaining ten days of the journey the old routine returned. Every morning Sam would have breakfast then go into the hold to feed and clean out Bess and then the monkey enclosure. When not needed for duties on deck he would sit with the monkeys, sometimes for hours just looking at them; the monkeys would sit and look back. Sam wondered what they were thinking, their mood had definitely become more hostile. No playfulness, no chattering, just sitting, not a sound. The only interruption would be when Sam gave the monkeys their evening feed. The mood had changed, they travelled in a brooding silence.

It was a late-night arrival at Harwich and although Sam was keen to get back to Tollesbury he decided he wouldn't unload his precious cargo until early the following morning. By six o'clock Bess and the wagon complete with three monkeys had been unloaded and were ready to go. Not keen on letting people see his mysterious cargo until he was ready to show off his monkeys, Sam covered the sides with tarpaulins secured top to bottom with ropes. By six thirty it had started to rain, he had left Harwich behind and was well on his way. Not even the rain could spoil the happiness he felt being back in England and on his way home with his precious Greenback monkeys.

Bess, now fully recovered from the snake bite was pleased to be out on firm ground and the open road, even if the load was heavy. To ease her burden Sam walked alongside the wagon for some of the time and they took a slow, steady pace. He had calculated that it would take about twelve hours to get to Tollesbury allowing for Bess to have several breaks along the way. This would mean that it might be getting dark for the last part of the journey along Old Ford Lane.

This didn't worry him too much, it was an area he knew well and a road he had travelled many times before. His only one small concern would be passing by the Creeks End Inn. The inn was an old, rough and rather rundown establishment, notorious for accommodating groups of smugglers and vagabonds who would silently arrive and depart under the cover of night as the tide ebbed and flowed up and down the creek. Sam reassured himself that as it would be early evening, if they were there they would probably be too busy drinking to take any notice of him as he passed by and with the tarpaulins covering the wagon he hoped he would look just like any number of farm workers who passed by during the day.

By mid-morning the rain had stopped, the sun came out and everything was well with the world. Every two hours he stopped to give Bess a break and to check on the monkeys, who continued to be very subdued. The tarpaulin was pulled up to allow fresh air to enter the cage and Sam gave the monkeys a handful of fruit and nuts each to eat. As he did he couldn't help but think of the one he had lost and that made him sad, but then he would look at the three he had and everything would seem a bit better. At least he had three good healthy monkeys, he would think.

In his mind Sam was planning the next stage of this

adventure; he imagined how surprised and pleased his parents would be when he arrived home with the Greenbacks. He was now so close, he would be home in a matter of hours. Sam smiled; these were going to be happy days. As he rode or walked alongside Bess he whistled and sang quietly to himself; his only regret was not having his good friend Baccary with him.

Just as dusk was falling they turned onto Old Ford Lane. Sam could see the notorious Creeks End Inn in the distance. It looked quiet. He checked the tarpaulin, ensuring it covered the cage completely, then climbed onto the wagon and drove Bess onwards. It had been a long day and Bess wasn't going as fast as Sam would have liked, but they were nearly home. Sam drove on. As he approached the inn he could see nobody about, it looked empty. Suddenly, when he was just twenty yards from the front door a man appeared as if from nowhere. He was scruffily dressed with ill-fitting black trousers, a long beige coat that was frayed at the cuffs and a dirty red scarf wrapped around his neck over what was probably once a white shirt. From each ear there hung a single gold hoop earring. He had a rough, unshaven appearance. Sam had seen men like him before, most notably when he was attacked on the night his faced was scarred. The man who stood in front of him now was probably only in his thirties although he looked much older. Most prominent was his large hooked nose and his long, almost white hair. He also appeared to only have half a set of front teeth. It didn't worry Sam too much; he had had to deal with far rougher and far bigger men in the past. The stranger stood in the middle of the road front of Bess. Sam didn't tell Bess to stop, but drove on, albeit slowly, and as Bess drew level with the man he took hold of her bridle and brought her to a halt.

"What have you got in the wagon, boy?" said the rough-looking stranger.

Sam knew he had to be confident and at the top of his voice he roared, "Nothing for you. Clear off out of my way!"

Sam quickly repeated himself, "I said CLEAR OFF, or do I need to get down from this wagon? Then you'll be sorry." Sam could see no one else in sight so one on one this man would be no problem for him.

"Steady on," said the stranger, "I don't want no trouble. I only want to warn you."

Sam was suspicious. "Warn me of what?"

The man smiled a toothless grin. "I'm trying to be helpful, lad, there's nobody here as there're all down the road trying to clear up after a tree come down and blocked the road."

Sam paused. "Is there no way past?"

"No, completely blocked, they have got every man trying to shift it."

Sam was suspicious. "Why are you not there?" he asked.

"I was told to stay here and divert people down the old sea wall path," he replied. "Just doing my duty." Again he smiled a toothless grin.

"The old sea wall path," repeated Sam. "Last time I travelled down that path it was a right rickety old state. Are you sure?"

"Look," said the man, "I'm trying to do you favour, take it or leave it." And with that he released his hold on Bess's bridle and pushed her away as he stepped back into the doorway from which he had appeared.

Sam thought for a moment. What should he do? Was the man telling the truth? Would the road still be blocked? If it was and he had to turn back it would be so late and he would then have to take the old path in complete darkness. That would be difficult. He really wanted to get home and if the road was blocked the quickest way would be the old path. He was now so close to home, no more than a mile, maybe a mile and a half, he thought, so he turned the wagon and set out down the old sea wall path.

He had been tricked and lied to!

The scruffy man who had stepped out in front of him was the leader of a rather nasty gang of smugglers and his men were not helping clear the road, they were instead waiting in hiding on the old sea wall path for any unsuspecting person who their boss could convince to take that path as night was falling.

DEATH ON THE SEA WALL

S am knew the path well and he knew it was very rough in places and great care was needed. However, he was in a hurry and very keen to get home.

Half a mile down the path three men waited, around a sharp bend hidden from sight. They were a ragged group of men, their clothes were well worn out and dirty, not one of them had a full set of teeth and they were all unshaven with straggly long hair. The men had all experienced and lived through a harsh life. They were armed; between them they had three daggers, two old steel swords and one hand gun. They were not the sort of people you would want to meet on a quiet coastal path especially as it was getting dark. Earlier the men had dug a trench across the path and covered it with branches and leaves ready to snag the wheels of any wagon or cart being driven over it by an unsuspecting driver, and now as darkness was falling they waited. As they waited they shared a bottle of rum, passed in turn to each other and drank straight from the bottle. They knew what they were waiting for… they were waiting for any lone traveller that their boss had tricked into taking the path and on that night, that lone traveller was Sam.

Bess, Sam and the wagon trundled on as darkness was falling, all the time getting closer and closer to the waiting group of vagabonds and thieves.

Suddenly Bess stumbled as her hooves fell into the trench. She managed to stay on her feet and stagger forward only to pull the front wheels of the wagon into the trench. This caused the wagon to come to an abrupt stop; one of the front wheels broke away from its axle and the whole wagon toppled over onto its side and slid down the embankment into the mud. Bess reared up and luckily broke free from her harness just as the wagon rolled down the slope. If the harness had not snapped under the strain the heavy wagon would have rolled on top of Bess and quite possibly killed her. Sam jumped clear. The men hiding behind the bushes jumped out and ran to the back of the wagon to grab what they thought would be the spoils of their crime. Sam ran to stop them, but he was pushed to the ground by two of the men and as he went to stand up he heard the shot and then felt the shearing pain as a bullet tore through the flesh at the top of his arm, throwing him to the ground again. As he lay on the ground what he saw next would scar his memory forever and that was to be a long, long time.

The door of the cage had become broken as the wagon rolled over and as the villains looked on it swung open and the three monkeys jumped out. The men stopped instantly, surprised and frozen by what was the last thing they were expecting to see. What happened next was worse. The men, frightened by what they saw, raised their daggers and swords and ran at the monkeys. "Kill 'em, kill 'em all!" they shouted. The man holding the gun raised and pointed it directly towards the biggest creature. Sam with all the strength he could muster jumped to his feet and threw himself towards the man, barging him aside. As he did so the gun fired, narrowly missing its intended victim. Then it happened; even now Sam can't be sure what he saw, but these men were no match for the monkeys. The monkeys had such agility and strength beyond belief. With ease the biggest monkey took hold of the man that had tried to shoot him and threw him an unbelievable thirty feet into the salt marsh. In a similar fashion the other two villains were dispatched. As the men wallowed in the mud of the marsh the monkeys went in after them. The men struggle to escape, but the monkeys kept pulling them back, then they would let the men scramble away again before again pulling them back. They were playing with them. As Sam watched he could see the men were becoming exhausted and then things turned nasty. As Sam looked on the monkeys started pulling at one of the men who was obviously in great pain and screaming. The monkeys were going to kill him, they were going to literally pull him apart. Their behaviour was similar to that which Sam had observed when a pack of lions had caught an antelope. They would pull the animal apart before eating it. But these were his loving and friendly monkeys, not killers. Or so he thought.

"NO, NO, stop!" shouted Sam. They didn't stop. Sam ran to the wagon and retrieved the revolver from its secret compartment and fired it twice over the monkeys' heads. Again he shouted, "Stop!" This time they did. They stopped, turned and looked at him. But they looked different, their eyes had turned fiery red and their lips were curled up exposing a flash of fierce white teeth. Sam could tell just by their body language that he needed to leave and he needed to leave fast. The three Greenbacks left their four assailants for dead swallowed up in the mud of the salt marsh and made their move towards him.

Without taking his eyes off the monkeys he could see Bess in the corner of his eye five paces to his right. As if she knew exactly what to do Bess moved towards Sam. In an instant Sam jumped astride Bess, took hold of her mane and galloped away with the troop of Greenbacks in hot pursuit. With blood streaming down from the wound in his arm which for the first time since he was shot was now causing considerable pain, he galloped towards his father's blacksmith forge and the safety of home less than half a mile from the path. After five minutes of hard riding he stopped to look over his shoulder. It had started to rain and the darkness of the night was complete, but in the distance he could see, he wasn't sure at first, but he could see and what he could see was getting nearer. In the darkness three pairs of bright red eyes were clearly moving towards him.

"C'mon, Bess, let's go." Bess reared up and leapt to the gallop again, into the darkness and the rain. But wait. Sam's mind was racing. What was he doing? If these monkeys were as fierce and as dangerous as he now believed, the last thing he should do is lead them to his parents' front door. It was too late now, the forge was directly in front of him. He leapt off Bess, opened the door to the forge where he and Bess hurried in, bolting the door behind them. Panting and in pain Sam leant back against the door and stared through the crack in the frame. Outside he saw them coming, the three of them marching purposely straight towards the forge. Quickly he barricaded the door as best as he could and waited. Within minutes the Greenbacks were banging on the door; they couldn't get in. Sam thought quickly, he must keep their attention; they mustn't wander round to the house. So he started shouting. "C'mon, monkeys, come and get me!" and with that he hammered on the door with an iron bar that was lying nearby. It worked; they continued to focus on the door. Sam hoped that no one in his parents' house could hear him and breathed a sigh of relief when after some time everything went quiet. Sam looked out through the crack and he could see the monkeys sitting exhausted ten feet from the door. He was thankful of the chance to catch his breath. What was he going to do? He must draw the Greenbacks away from the house.

He was able to dress his wound with some clean muslin bandages that his father kept in a box for dealing with occasional injuries. Although it was extremely painful, once he had cleaned it up it didn't look too bad. "I'll live," he said to himself. He dozed through the night, but he knew what he would do at first light. Before the sun rose he had fed and saddled

Bess; he was ready. When the first rays of light appeared though the cracks in the door and while the Greenbacks lay sleeping Sam threw open the doors and galloped out on Bess, pausing only to wake the monkeys with a slash of his whip to rouse them into following him. Then he galloped off back towards the docks at Harwich. The monkeys had no chance of keeping up with Bess and as they passed the salt marshes Sam could see the Greenbacks stop and disappear from sight, camouflaged as their green and brown fur blended with the marsh. Sam stopped and looked; he had lost them, he had escaped. He continued on his way to Harwich.

Back at the house Sam's father had been woken by a noise coming from the forge. He looked out and saw what looked like Sam and Bess galloping into the distance followed by three strange-looking creatures that he did not recognise, or were his eyes deceiving him? Without waking his wife he dressed and left the house, walking in the direction he thought Sam had taken, towards the salt marsh. It wasn't long before he came across the wreckage of a wagon. The tide had washed over the remains during the night, taking much of the wooden structure of the wagon out to sea and what was left was covered with mud. Still visible in the mud were two wheels, one was complete and the other was broken with only a few of its original spokes remaining. There were also some iron bars protruding out of the mud. Lying face down in the mud close by was a section of wooden board. Sam's father lifted it out of the mud and turned it over, and with his hand he wiped the mud from it; it wasn't complete, but written clearly in red letters on what remained were the words – 'World famous showman'. Sam's father looked at it for a second and then threw it back into the mud. He had no idea what had gone on there during the night or what had happened to Sam, but he knew that whatever he had found he must keep it to himself – no one must ever know.

He walked on until he came across fragments of clothes and what looked like, he wasn't sure, but it could be bodies, three bodies. The tide had covered them and whatever the remains were, they were slowly drifting out to sea on the ebb tide. They couldn't be the remains of Sam, he thought, for he was certain he had seen him early that morning galloping into the distance on Bess. He was certain he was alive, but what had happened?

Sam's father returned home; it was a mystery, made even more mysterious when later that evening Bess returned to the forge. Sam's father recognised Bess immediately and before anyone else in the house could see her he took her to a neighbouring farm owned by a close friend. He made him promise not to tell anyone about Bess and to keep her safe until Sam returned, as he hoped he would, but had no idea when. Sam's father never mentioned it again, the secret he kept to himself. He never spoke of it, never told Sam's mother and he was not to see Sam again for another ten years.

It was a mystery. What had happened? The only clue was a drunken rogue with a hooked nose and long white hair, who would tell people a ridiculous story, that he had seen green fiery monsters come out of the salt marsh and eat his friends. No one believed him, no one except for Sam's father. But he said nothing.

THE BEST AND

THE WORST DAY

By mid-morning Sam had reached Harwich. It was going to be his escape route, he needed to get away. He had just witnessed three men murdered by a group of monkeys that he had brought onto the Saltings. If the authorities were able to link the monkeys to Sam he would surely be found guilty of bringing the animals into the country and he would be hung. At the gates to the dock and with a heavy heart, he set Bess free. "Run, Bess. Run home." And he pushed Bess away. Having been his constant companion for so long, she hesitated and stopped. Sam thought that she wouldn't go but then the roar of a ship's horn spooked her enough to send her on her way. Her return home to the forge only added to the mystery. Where was Sam?

Sam knew what he was going to do. If he could just find Captain Anderson and his ship the *Sea Eagle* he would ask for a job. He was sure that the captain would take him as part of the crew. But what story would he tell him about the Greenbacks? It didn't matter, he was too late, for as he walked through the gates he could see the *Sea Eagle* slipping past the fairway buoys and heading out to sea.

Plan B, he thought. What was plan B? Plan B was to hide in the docks and rest for a while and then under the cover of dark he would stow away on one of the ships, but which one? The docks never stopped working, but at night they did get a lot quieter. Sam just needed to find the right ship. He was looking for one that traded with the near continent, Holland, Belgium or France. He couldn't hide away at sea for too long, he hadn't eaten anything since the day before and he had a bullet wound to his shoulder which was becoming ever more painful. If he could be ashore in Europe by tomorrow night he would be safe, he could find somewhere to stay and get some food, have his wound stitched and make a plan. His mind was spinning, but he had no clear idea of what to do, all he could think was that he needed to get away.

He saw his chance, a fine-looking vessel that looked like it had finished loading and was ready to leave on the early morning tide. The ship was called the *Queen Anne* and registered in London. Sam chose his moment well; he waited until the crew were asleep and the night watchman was dozing, when he crept up the gang plank and onto the lower deck. Along the deck on each side of the ship were the lifeboats, three either side. He lifted the tarpaulin cover on the first one he came across, jumped in and pulled the tarpaulin back over the boat. Safe at last, at least for a while. His next problem wouldn't be until he needed to get ashore. He settled himself down and fell into a deep relaxed sleep.

He woke in pain; the movement of the ship and the hard wooden floor he was sleeping on had aggravated his wound, but from the movement he could tell they were away at sea. He carefully lifted the tarpaulin and looked out; as far as he could see, all he could see was the sea. *Can't be long now until we dock,* and with that thought he settled down in the bottom of the lifeboat to plan his next move. Then a pain in his stomach reminded him, he was starving and hadn't eaten for days. Still, it took his mind off the pain in his arm where a little over twenty-four hours ago he was shot! Things would be better now, he had time to plan, and after all it couldn't get much worse.

It got worse. As night fell the ship still hadn't docked as Sam had expected. They were still at sea. The sun rose on his second day, they were still at sea. He hadn't eaten or drunk anything for three days and his throat was painfully dry. In the bottom of the lifeboat on which he was hiding he discovered a small pool of rainwater that had leaked through the tarpaulin. It tasted stale and bracken, but it did ease the pain in his throat. Now it was just the pain in his shoulder and the hunger pains in his stomach he needed to do something about. Sam tried to mentally calculate where they were and where they could be going and when was he going to have his next meal. He could tell by the position of the sun that they were heading west. Surely they would dock soon, he was now very hungry.

Another day went by, still no sign of land. Then later that afternoon he heard two of the crew talking near to where he was hiding. They spoke of what sounded like Bombay and India Gate. Sam wasn't sure he heard correctly; Bombay was India, surely they weren't going to India. He would die of starvation long before they arrived there. Then he clearly heard one of the men shout, "How long to Cape Town, Skipper?"

"With a fair wind we'll be there in six weeks," replied the skipper.

"Six weeks." Sam stifled a gasp for fear of being detected. He couldn't live for six weeks in the ship's lifeboat, if he didn't die from starvation he was sure his shoulder would become infected and kill him. He needed a survival plan, but first he had to eat. Sam was desperate to eat so as soon as it became dark he crept out from his hiding place and silently made his way along the deck. He was directed by the smell of freshly baked bread coming from the ship's galley. He could see a light in the galley window and as he lifted his head to see through the window he could see a line of bread rolls cooling, fresh out of the oven. *Be careful,* he thought. *Now's not the time to be careless.* He had heard how on some ships stowaways when caught were often thrown overboard and nobody would ever know. If he could take two or three of the rolls that would keep him fed for a couple of days at least. When he felt the moment was right, Sam on his hands and knees entered the galley and hid under the bench below where the bread rolls were cooling. He sneaked a look around to ensure it was all clear and then stretched his arm up to the top of the bench and with his fingers started to blindly search for the rolls. At that moment the head chef entered the galley carrying a sharp butcher's hatchet. On seeing a hand stealing his freshly cooked roll, he brought the hatchet down full force onto the bench, severing the top of Sam's middle finger and index finger on his left hand.

"How dare you steal my rolls?" screamed the chef.

Sam just screamed and then fainted. At the same time the ship's captain was taking a stroll along the deck with his youngest daughter Esme, who by chance was accompanying him on this trip. It was her first time at sea as she wanted to accompany her father; she was feeling very low as her mother had just died. She had been ill for some time and Esme had been looking after her. She had read every medical book she could find and consulted every doctor in the area but was unable to save her mother's life. She died peacefully at home with Esme and her father by her side. They had a small funeral attended by friends from the village and a couple of cousins that they had rarely seen before. Her father's ship, which was moored at Harwich, was due to set sail; it had already been delayed to allow time for the funeral, and it couldn't be delayed any longer. The sympathetic owners had offered to put a replacement captain onboard to allow Captain Brodie a chance to stay at home and take a few months off. But there was no way the captain was going to allow someone else to take command of his ship. And there was no way he was going to leave Esme at home on her own. So it was decided she had best come with him to India. Once there they would stay with her brother, who had been unable to get home for the funeral in time and she hadn't seen for some time. Several years before, having completed his training to become a doctor, he had moved to India with his new wife and now lived and worked in Bombay.

The captain on hearing the scream ran into the galley quickly followed by his daughter.

"What's going on?" he demanded.

His daughter on seeing Sam in such a dishevelled state and with blood pouring from his hand, without hesitation shouted at one of the crew to quickly fetch her the first aid kit and as other crew members arrived she instructed them to carry Sam to the empty cabin next to hers.

The captain was not altogether certain this was the right course of action. He was not accustomed to giving stowaways their own cabin on his ship. He wanted some explanation as to what Sam was doing there. However, he could tell that his young daughter who had always displayed quite a forceful and determined personality was not going to be overruled, so on this occasion he decided the best course of action was to stand back.

Fate, strangely sometimes can make the worst day of your life lead to the best, and without the worst the best would never have of happened. This was the case for Sam.

He didn't know how long he had been unconscious, but when he opened his eyes he knew something different had happened. It was like dream, he was in a bed with sheets and a pillow, he appeared to be wearing a clean white night shirt, the wound where he was shot was dressed with a new clean bandage and there was a glass of water by his bed. It wasn't just that it was water, he hadn't drunk from a glass for a long, long time and it's surprising how such little things can make such a difference. If it hadn't been for the excruciating pain coming from his heavily bandaged left hand he would have thought he was in heaven. In fact he wasn't sure he was not in heaven, everything was still very hazy and when Esme the captain's daughter entered the room appearing like a vision of an angel, that confirmed it, he must have died and this must be heaven. He drifted into unconsciousness again. This didn't last as he was abruptly woken by intense pain coming from his left hand. "What happening?" he moaned. "Stop, stop, I thought heaven would be painless."

"Don't be such a baby," said Esme as she gently redressed the bandages on his hand.

Sam tried to struggle but all strength had left him, he hadn't realised what a toll the last days had taken on his body. He just lay there barely able to speak and unable to move; he had never felt so weak.

Esme produced a bowl of soup which she fed to Sam, as even with his good right hand he lacked the strength to hold a spoon. Later that day she appeared again, with food. This happened at regular intervals throughout the day. By the third day Sam's strength had recovered enough for him to take in more of what was happening. He was in a ship's cabin, he had no idea how he got there or what the ship was called or where it was going. Who was the beautiful girl with the long fair hair and blue eyes that kept appearing to feed him and change his bandages? He really concentrated and tried to remember what had happened. He remembered the monkeys, Greenbacks, he had caught them in Africa. Then he remembered the wagon, the pain of being shot, the monkeys chasing him and Bess. Where was Bess?

"Where am I and who are you?" he asked as Esme entered the room.

"Well you're looking brighter," she replied. "You're on the *Queen Anne*, my father's the captain, Captain Brodie, and my name is Esme. What's your name?"

"Sam, Sam Shine, how did I get here?" answered Sam.

"I have no idea how you got onboard the *Queen Anne* or where you had come from. When I first saw you, you were looking in a very sorry state. You had a wound to your arm where you had been shot, and you clearly hadn't eaten or washed from some time and the chef had just cut off the tips of your middle and index fingers. We thought you were going to die and I had to beg my father not to throw you overboard. Did someone attack you?"

Sam said nothing. There was nothing he could say as he could barely remember himself. He thought he best wait a few days to try and find a story that Esme might believe. He didn't have to wait long. The following morning Esme came to his room again, this time with her father, Captain Brodie. Sam tried to stand but he couldn't, he just collapsed back onto the bed.

"Take it easy, lad," said the captain. "Now tell me, why should I not throw you overboard?" The captain had been at sea many years and had a rugged appearance and abrupt manner; he was probably in his fifties and smartly dressed in the uniform of a ship's captain, but it was a manner that Sam recognised. He had met many captains and he understood them and their responsibility to the ship and crew and they didn't take kindly to stowaways. But Captain Brodie had the look and manner of what Sam recognised to be a very experienced and very good captain. *This is a fair man,* thought Sam. *I should be safe for now.* Esme had clearly saved his life, at least for the time being.

Sam thought quickly and told the captain what he could remember, or at least what he thought it best to tell. He told the assembled group how he had just returned from Africa on the ship the *Sea Eagle.* They had docked at Harwich. He said how on leaving the docks he was attacked by a group of men who stole all of his possessions. He recognised them as being members of the crew from a ship that he had crossed paths with in Madeira some time ago. They had stolen goods from a ship they were crewing which they were then trying to sell in the market. He had caught them and reported it to the captain. He knew that if he had not reported, the men the whole crew from that particular ship would be punished. Sam could never have stood by and let that happen especially when he knew the truth. They were not good men and the captain was pleased to get rid of them when they had docked at Harwich a few hours earlier than the *Sea Eagle*. When they spotted Sam coming ashore they made a plan to ambush him, beat him and throw him into the sea. After a struggle Sam managed to break free and escaped from their clutches and run away as fast as he could. As he did so, one of the men shot at him, hitting him in his right shoulder. He staggered up onto the first gang plank he came across, climbed under the tarpaulin of a lifeboat and hid.

Esme, almost in tears threw her arms around him. "You poor man. You're safe now, we'll look after you."

The captain said nothing. He paused, looked hard at Sam and left. Sam knew it was a lie, but he didn't think anyone would believe the truth.

A day later the captain came to see him again to say that one of his crew had come to speak to him. He said that a few years ago he served on the crew of the *Sea Eagle* under Captain Anderson and he said Sam was the first mate.

"Is that true?" he asked.

"Yes, who was it?" asked Sam.

"Billy Bones," replied the captain.

Sam could hardly believe it. "What, Billy is on board here?" he asked with a delighted smile. "I haven't seen Bill for ages." Sam relaxed; he knew Billy well, ever since the incident in Hamburg nearly six years ago. Billy would certainly be able to vouch for him.

"Did you serve on the *Sea Eagle*?" asked the captain.

"Yes sir, I was first mate, I know Captain Anderson well. I was on his ship returning from Africa and I would have been on it again given half a chance."

"Hmm." The captain seemed to be considering his options. "Let's see what we can do." And with that, he left.

Esme, who had been present throughout, smiled and Sam felt quite relieved. There was someone on board who could vouch for him, he would be alright.

"Don't worry, Sam, I'm sure everything will be alright," said Esme.

"That's fine for you to say," Sam replied quickly. "You're not sitting here with the tops of your fingers missing, a gunshot wound to your arm and no money in your pockets." The realisation of his situation was starting to hit home. What had he done? What was he going to do? There were times when he had even considered throwing himself off the ship. Sam lay back on his bed and shut his eyes.

Esme left the cabin, saying, "I think you should stop sulking and consider how lucky you are." She slammed the door.

It must have been the sudden noise of the door slamming that made Sam sit up; straight away he knew she was right, he was lucky, no man could ever have been luckier. Esme was the nicest, sweetest person he had ever met.

The ship sailed on and every day without fail Esme would come and dress Sam's wounds and every day they would speak more of their families, friends and homes. Sam spoke about his mother and father, the forge and his grandfather's church. But it was when he spoke about Bess that Esme's eyes lit up. They both loved and missed their horses, Sam's Bess and Esme's Star. Esme's horse was called Star, naturally, because of the white star on her forehead. They spoke about how once settled they would really love to have another horse and how it would be almost impossible to replace the ones they had left behind. Esme told Sam how her big brother was a doctor who had married and moved to India to work as physician to the families of the wealthy Indian merchants. She was really interested in medicine and had read and studied hard. However, opportunities for young women to train as doctors in England were few and far between.

She had worked as a nurse in her local hospital and had learnt that there was a real need for medical staff in India and that was what she was going to do. Much to her mother's disapproval; she had already lost her son to India – she didn't want to lose her daughter too. But now her mother was gone it seemed it was meant to be. Sam just felt pleased to have been so well looked after and was thankful that Esme had a good knowledge of medicine.

As Sam's condition improved he was visited again by the captain.

"Listen, lad," said the captain. "I've got no time, no time at all for stowaways. But I'm not known for throwing people overboard." He looked at Sam just like Sam's father would look at him when he was about to have stern words with him. The captain was about the same age and build as his father and had a similar serious personality.

"I have thought about your situation," said the captain sternly. "I need an extra deck hand, can you do it?"

"Yes sir."

"Very well, now I'm giving you a chance, one chance, but you put one foot wrong, just one, and this could all change. Do you understand?"

"Yes sir," was all Sam could say.

"We're going to Bombay in India. We shall be stopping in Cape Town for supplies in a few weeks, report to me tomorrow morning at eight." And with that, he turned and left the room.

The following morning Sam reported for duty as instructed. Esme had washed and patched his clothes, Sam had washed and shaved. All in all he didn't look too bad all things considered. He paused outside the captain's cabin, took a deep breath and knocked on the door and without waiting to be invited in he entered the room. Esme was already there talking to her father.

"Morning sir, morning Esme," said Sam as he went to sit down.

"Don't sit, Mr Shine," said the captain. "Listen, one of my officers has been taken unwell, so ill that we are going to have to stop and put him ashore somewhere safe for him to receive better medical attention. That leaves me short of one officer."

"Yes sir, I can do that," interrupted Sam.

"Well maybe," said the captain. "I'm unsure about you and to be honest I'm not sure I like you. You're brash, foolhardy, far too confident and you smile too much. But, I will give you a fair chance. You've got a week. Prove yourself to me and the job is yours, if not we'll set you ashore with my sick officer. I've got no time to support idle stowaways. You can keep your cabin, but as I said yesterday, one mistake, just one, and you are off this ship so fast you'll be praying there is land nearby." And with that, the captain looked at Esme and said, "Are you happy now?"

Esme just smiled.

The captain then turned to Sam who was standing speechless and barked, "Don't stand there doing nothing, lad. Go, go. The first mate will give you instructions."

"I won't let you down, sir, I promise."

With that, Sam left the room, smiled and thought to himself, *She must really like me.*

He wasn't wrong, that's for sure and for his part, he thought she was the most beautiful girl he had ever set eyes on.

To cut a long story short, Sam kept true to his word and worked as hard as he had ever done. By the end of the week the sick officer had been set ashore in Madeira for medical treatment and by the end of the second week his position on board was secure. Even the captain was beginning to like him. By the end of the third week his relationship with Esme had strengthened; every off-duty hour they spent together. By the time the ship reached Cape Town they were talking about their future together. When they arrived at Bombay it had been decided, Esme would ask her brother if Sam could stay with them. Then Sam would find a job working at one of the English trading companies based there. But first Sam had to speak to the captain, he had something else really important to ask. What Sam had to ask didn't come as a surprise, the whole crew suspected it including the captain. However, he wasn't going to make it too easy for Sam. Sam knocked on his door and entered. "Have you got a moment, sir?" he asked.

"What, lad? I'm really busy, make it quick, what do you want?" the captain said abruptly.

Sam was nervous, but undeterred by the captain's manner. He quickly said what he wanted to say. "Please may I have permission to marry Esme?"

"WHAT? What did you say?"

"I want to marry Esme," repeated Sam. "She is the most beautiful and caring person I've ever met and I love her."

"WHAT? What?" said the captain again. "What has a lad like you got to offer her? Do you have any money or any prospects? No, you have nothing!"

Sam's heart sank. He looked at the captain who was standing with his back to him. The room fell silent and after what seemed like an age but was probably no more than a couple of seconds, the captain turned to face Sam with the biggest smile on his face that Sam had ever seen. He took Sam's hand and shook it vigorously. "Congratulations, lad. Sit down, let's talk." Sam was speechless. The captain went on to explain how he had observed how happy the couple had made each other and how much of a hard worker Sam was. As far as the captain was concerned it didn't matter that Sam had nothing; hard work and the ability to make the most of situations you find yourself in were skills that Sam had in abundance. Finally, he had to own up to the fact that Esme had spoken to him the previous evening and told him how much she loved Sam. Her happiness was everything to him. So it was agreed, they would be married before the *Queen Anne* set sail back to England. The only regret was that Esme's mother had passed away a year earlier and never had the chance to meet Sam.

For just a short moment in time, all concerns over the Greenback monkeys, Baccary and his parents back in Tollesbury had been pushed to the back of Sam's mind. It would not be forever!

THE CALL OF HOME

Esme's brother James and his wife Emma welcomed them with open arms. Esme had got to know Emma well before she left with her brother for India. And while the two women planned the wedding, James took Sam and introduced him to several English traders based in Bombay. It wasn't long before Sam had secured a position with a cotton trader. His job was to oversee the loading of the cotton onto the ships.

Four weeks after arriving in Bombay and five months after they first met, the wedding took place. A brilliant day by all accounts only saddened by Esme's father having to set sail for England two days later.

Life in India was good for Sam and Esme. Soon they had found their own house just outside of the main town on the coast road overlooking the sea. It was a one-storey bungalow with more rooms than they would ever need, all set in its own large grounds. It was so different to what he was used to in Tollesbury; the weather was incredibly hot most of the year and when it was not incredibly hot there was torrential rain. No matter how different it was, every evening as he sat on the veranda and looked out over the sea he couldn't stop himself thinking of home. He had written to his parents every week since he had arrived in Bombay; they were relieved to hear from him. Letters could take from four to six months to be delivered to England.

He told his parents about Esme and how lovely she was. He told them how her mother had died and how she really wanted to become a doctor like her brother and how her brother had found a position for Esme in the local hospital nursing sick children which she loved. He told them all about his job working with the cotton traders and of all the ships that regularly arrived from England. He described their house overlooking the sea on the coast road outside the main town. Finally, he would write about how much he missed them, Bess and Tollesbury.

His mother wrote back to him with an update on family, local and national news. She didn't often mention the salt marsh, but on two occasions she did, only to dismiss "silly talk" she had heard about mystery animals seen living there and to comment on how people rarely visited the marshes.

His father wrote once to say how Baccary had come looking for him and how his father had told him about discovering the smashed up wagon on the salt marsh and how he had no idea what had happened. He told Baccary about seeing Sam gallop away from the forge earlier that morning and how Bess had returned later that day on her own. He also said how he had kept the secret and told nobody about the wrecked wagon and seeing Sam. Baccary didn't say, but he knew what had happened. And this was further confirmed when he heard people in the village talking about the mysterious events that had happened on the marshes; animals that had gone missing, bird life that was disappearing and rumours of sightings of green furry monsters with fiery red eyes. All stories were usually dismissed as tall tales. Baccary stayed some time at the forge in Tollesbury and worked alongside Sam's father. He was there when his parents received the first letter from Sam. He was there as Sam's mother cried with relief. He wasn't there the day after the letter had arrived, he had gone. He had gone to find Sam in Bombay.

By the time Baccary arrived in Bombay Sam had

been away from England for just over a year. Since the incident on the path in Tollesbury he had travelled to India, met and married the love of his life, found good well-paid employment, bought a house and he and Esme were expecting their first child. He was a world away from the young adventurer he used to be and the Greenback monkeys. Despite all of what Baccary had to say, he was not going to return to Tollesbury, he couldn't. How could he leave everything he had? He would have to live with the consequences of his actions but at that moment in time there was nothing he could do. It was not an easy decision, it played on his mind constantly and often kept him awake at night and it continued to do so for many years. Baccary understood; he had found Esme to be as lovely and charming as anyone he had ever met. If it was he that was married to Esme, if it was his child she was carrying, he would not leave either, he told Sam. The men agreed that the time was not right. They would wait and see what happened.

Baccary was interested in the work Sam was doing as a cotton trader. He often accompanied him to his office and was quick to pick up on how the business worked. Two months after arriving in Bombay, Baccary left with plans to set up a trading post on the Gold Coast, his home country. It was a sad farewell, but it would not be forever and it would not be their last. The bond between the two men would only become stronger.

Sam's employment was proving to be very successful and by the time he was thirty years old he had become a partner in the Bombay cotton and silk trading company. By the time they were celebrating his thirty-fourth birthday, he and Esme had two young children, a boy and girl, Charlotte and George. Both born in February two years apart, Charlotte was the eldest. Esme's father was a frequent visitor, or as frequent as the long voyage from England to India could be. The *Queen Anne* being loaded with cotton and silk was a regular sight in the docks.

In those quiet moments when nothing much was happening and everything was peaceful, Sam's thoughts would often turn to Tollesbury, his parents and Bess. Esme's father would always bring Sam news from his family who he visited whenever he was in Harwich and as Sam thought they might, Captain Brodie and his father had become good friends. However, the news Sam was receiving was not what he wanted to hear. Life in Tollesbury was not as bright as he would have expected for the thriving village he had left all those years ago. There was something there that nobody spoke openly about, something that scared people, something that had stopped the locals going about their business in the carefree way they had always previously done. Sheep grazing on the salt marsh had disappeared, chickens and family pets had gone missing. Anything untoward that happened was attributed to the strange creatures roaming the salt marshes at night, frightening anyone they came across. It was said that they had great strength, bright red eyes and green fur. Some also reported seeing them breathe fire like medieval dragons. This was very convenient to any thieves who were working locally! These stories according to the letters he had received from his parents were not always believed but they had affected the lives of the small community that lived there. Sam knew the truth and he knew the truth was his fault. For it was him that had brought the monsters there and it was him that had run away and left them there. He knew he must go back and deal with it, but how? What about Esme and the children? Should they come with him? Should he leave them behind in India? He just didn't know what to do and as he procrastinated days, weeks, months and then years passed.

Then surprise news came from her father. He arrived at their front door and sat himself down on the porch like he had done so many times before. Sam and

Esme sat with him; it was a fine evening with a cooling breeze coming off the sea. Out of the blue he suddenly announced that this was going to be his last trip, he had just turned sixty-five and he had had enough. His ship, the *Queen Anne*, was one of the last ships to be solely reliant on sail power; the steam ships were taking over. They were both faster and more efficient. He explained how it was now time to go. The ship's owners had invested a lot of money in buying new steam ships. They had decided to scrap the *Queen Anne* on her return to Harwich and had offered the captain a brand new steam ship to command. But it was not for him, it was the natural time for him to go, he planned to retire on his return to England. He had bought a small house overlooking the river at Wivenhoe and he felt the time had come to settle for the rest of his days there. He would not be coming back to India. Esme cried, Sam just sat holding her hand. They were very fond of the old captain. Suddenly Esme stood up from her chair. "Sam," she said, "we're going home." Both Sam and his father-in-law looked at Esme, but it was clear this was not something that needed to be discussed, it wasn't a "should we?" or "do you think?", it was a "we are." Esme had spoken. She was always very decisive.

"Well," said Sam, "that's what we shall do." The

timing was good; they had earned a reasonable amount of money from the very lucrative cotton and silk trade, enough to enable them to set up a comfortable home in England and Sam was sure there were going to be plenty of opportunities to use his contacts to continue his work once settled back home. Most importantly, Sam missed home, he missed his parents, Bess and the Saltings, and he wanted to be home. At last he would be able to do something about those monkeys.

They had a lot to do but by the time the *Queen Anne* was fully loaded the family had packed up their house and were ready to leave onboard the *Queen Anne*. Charlotte and George were only eight and six years old and very excited; it was going to be their first sea voyage and it was going to be with their granddad! It would only be Esme's second, the first being when she arrived. But for Sam, being back on a ship was a bit like being home already, and although not part of the crew he walked the decks like he was still a ranking officer. What nobody knew, not even Esme, was that he was making a plan, a plan to rid the salt marshes and Tollesbury of three very undesirable Greenback monkeys. There was just one thing that Sam could not get out of his mind. Just how old were these creatures and how long did they live for? India had plenty of monkeys and from his research he had learnt that they normally live between ten and fifteen years. He had been away for more than ten years, surely they were not still alive! But from the reports he had been receiving they were very much alive and kicking. But just how was he going to catch those monkeys?

Five months later at about 7am, the *Queen Anne* docked at Harwich. Sam and a very excited family couldn't wait to get ashore. Arrangements were made for a carriage to pick the family up from the dockside. Esme's father had a friend who owned warehouses by the docks and he had arranged for most of their luggage and belongings to be put into storage there until they had sorted out their more permanent accommodation. Initially Sam was sure they could all stay with his mother and father. Although his parents' house was small there was always a warm welcome for any visitors. They said their goodbyes to Esme's father, who still had more than enough work to do before he could finally retire, and just before midday set off on their way to Tollesbury. Sam had not had time to send a telegram to his parents to tell them he was coming home before they had set sail, however, he had left a note in his old office saying if a message should arrive from his parents wanting to know where he was, tell them he was on his way back to England. It was going to be quite a surprise for his parents, and it was.

The thirty-mile journey from Harwich to Tollesbury would take about eight hours; it probably would have been better to have waited until the following morning but Sam was keen to get home and Esme couldn't wait to meet Sam's family and see Tollesbury after hearing so much about it over the last ten years. The first part of the journey went well, but as they came nearer to their destination Sam became unusually quiet, deep in thought and remembering the last time he had travelled down the familiar roads he was now on. How the last time he was so full of hope, so pleased with himself to have brought the monkeys to Tollesbury and how proud his parents were to be of him when he arrived home with a family of three Greenback monkeys, just as he said he would do when he left. And then in a matter of minutes, how everything had changed. The wagon had rolled over, the monkeys had escaped, he had been shot, his attackers killed and he had fled without his parents ever knowing he had returned home. The only evidence of him ever being there was a smashed up wagon and a family of Greenback monkeys who for the last ten years, according to letters he had received from his mother, had haunted the village.

He was deep in thought. He knew what he had to do; it would be risky, but he had to rid Tollesbury of those monkeys and put right what he had done. Catching them was going to be difficult. The salt marshes extended for several miles in all directions, they were often cut off from the mainland at high tide and the monkeys were very secretive and elusive. He needed help and there was only one person he could think of who had the skills needed and he hadn't seen him for three years. Baccary. Where was Baccary? The last he had heard, Baccary was travelling overland to towards the eastern Mediterranean to help develop a new overland trade route. He needed to find him.

So Sam had done two things before leaving Bombay. Firstly, he had given instructions for all of their remaining possessions to be packed up and sent on the next available ship to Harwich where they would be put in temporary storage. Secondly, and most importantly he had engaged the services of an ex-soldier he had made acquaintance with to find Baccary. Although he had tried writing to Baccary on several occasions using the address he had given and that of the mission where Baccary had lived as a child, the only reply he had received was from a woman who Sam thought might have been Baccary's sister

Effi who had said he was travelling overland developing new trade routes. He gave the soldier a letter to hand Baccary once he found him. The letter was really a plea for help, he needed Baccary's help now almost as much as he did when Baccary saved his life in the jungle. He gave the soldier the address of the mission near Accra as a starting point and had promised a decent-size bonus if the solder could get Baccary to England before the summer had started the following year. He had already decided that if he was going to catch Greenbacks his best chance would be in the summer.

It was just after seven in the evening when the carriage carrying the young family arrived in Tollesbury. Sam's mother, father and now very elderly grandfather were just sitting down for their evening supper when they heard the sound of a carriage outside their house, not a sound they would normally hear, especially in the early evening. Annie went to the window to take a look. "What's all the noise about?" asked Jack, Sam's father.

"There's a grand-looking carriage outside with, it looks like a family in it, the children are very young, I don't know why they're here."

"They must be lost, poor souls, let's go outside

and see if we can help," said Grandfather. All three of them left the table and went outside. They stood looking at the carriage and addressed the well-dressed man standing with his back to them, helping a beautiful lady step out.

"Can we be of any help?" said Jack. The man he was addressing turned to face him.

For the rest of her life Annie would say that that day was the best day of her life except for the day her beautiful son was born. The day he returned home to stay with his beautiful wife and beautiful children.

Over the next few months Sam an Esme set about finding a new home for their family. With the money Sam had earned while working in India he had enough to purchase a rather pretty detached thatched cottage on the outskirts of the village. Not so small to be insignificant, but large enough to show that he was a person of importance. With his remaining money he bought into a company that operated warehouse storage at the Harwich docks. It was owned by a very old friend of Esme's father who had been looking for some time to find someone who would take over and allow him to become more of a silent partner and retire. The arrangement suited them both.

By Christmas that year the family were becoming

well established in the life of the village; Charlotte had even started at the local school. Of course her grandmother was the teacher. As for Sam, when he wasn't managing the warehouse business he was out on the salt marshes looking. A couple of times he thought he could see something but he couldn't be certain; he needed to get nearer, he needed a boat. Without a boat he couldn't be sure of finding the place where the elusive Greenbacks were living. He didn't tell Esme what he was doing, he didn't tell her about the boat and he didn't tell her about his fear that if the Greenbacks saw him they would come after him again. Sam tried speaking to the locals about the salt marsh, and whether anything strange had ever happened there. The most common response was, "Oh, we don't go down there, there's nothing to see on those marshes." Or, "Don't listen to tales about what happens down there, they're just silly superstitions." Regardless, the locals didn't go near the salt marshes and there was a general reluctance to talk about it and what was clear, no sheep or wildlife of any kind including birds could be seen. The place was cold, dark and desolate.

ACTION ON THE SALT MARSH

Christmas and New Year came and went, but there was no sign of Baccary. Where was he? Sam didn't even know if he was alive or dead and he hadn't heard a thing from the man he employed to find him. On top of that, Sam hadn't a clue how he was going to catch the monkeys, he couldn't even confirm where they lived on the marsh and the marsh was a big place. Had they moved on, maybe, moved inland, or were they indeed dead? He just didn't know. He continued looking, every spare moment when the tide was high he would be out on his boat. He needed to search every inch, he needed to be sure they were no longer there.

On a particularly cold day towards the end of January his questions were answered. Just as he had almost convinced himself they were either dead or had moved on, it happened. On an especially high spring tide that allowed him to enter an area of salt marsh he had not previously been able to reach. Just as he was about to turn for home something made him stop and take one last look around, then he saw it. He wasn't sure at first, he lay low in the boat and just let it drift, quietly using the occasional stroke of the oar to maintain position. He didn't want to get too close, the last thing he wanted was to be seen. For now he just needed to confirm that they were alive and where they lived. He was able to do both. He had hoped he would never find them, that they had died, been killed or moved on, anything that would mean he wouldn't have to do anything, but no, they were there, there was no way he could be mistaken, they were there. Strangely, they were just as he remembered them, two bigger ones he had always presumed to be the parents and a smaller one to be the child; they hadn't changed at all even though it had been ten years since he had last seen them. He thought to himself how similar they were. People had often commented to him that he never looked a day older. Maybe it was a bond between them.

Now he had just to plan his next move. *Where is Baccary?* he thought.

With the beginning of spring Sam was determined that with or without Baccary he had to do something.

He knew where they were and he knew how many of them there were and late one night a plan came into his mind. He was lying in bed unable to sleep, when his mind started to reflect on the day that he first arrived back in England with the Greenbacks all those years ago. He remembered travelling along Hall Lane and being apprehensive when passing the Creeks End Inn and then he focussed on the man who had tricked him into diverting down the old sea wall path instead of staying on the lane. The scruffy, rough-looking fellow with white hair, hooked nose and hardly any teeth, the gang leader and the only survivor of that terrible night. Could he be the man he needed to help him deal with the problem on the salt marsh? After all, it was the monkeys who took the lives of three of his men on that night. The following evening Sam would go to the Creeks End Inn to see if he could find him. Although he felt the chances of the man still being there after so many years were slight.

The Creeks End Inn was not a place honest people visited; it was quite run down and shabby, even worse than Sam had remembered. There was broken furniture piled up outside by a pile of logs and the front door looked like it would fall off its hinges at any minute. The inside was no better, the bar was made from roughly sawn planks of wood supported by two large barrels, one at each end. On top of the bar was another barrel lying on its side which presumably contained some local brand of ale. The furniture was battered and sparse, held together with nails and rope. Behind the bar were a couple of large bottles that looked like they may contain whiskey and gin. There was probably about half a dozen men mostly sitting on their own staring into their drinks. As Sam entered the bar he stood out like a sore thumb, all eyes turned to him, the well-dressed stranger and obvious gentleman. Sam walked up to the bar and asked for ale. The bartender place a tankard of ale in front of him but before letting it go he said, "State your business here, my friend, or leave now, while you can still stand."

Sam had been to some rough places in his time at sea, and there was nothing in that inn that was going to scare him. He laid a half gold sovereign down on the bar, looked the barman in the eye and stated his business. "I'm looking for the man with white hair, hooked nose and only a few decent teeth."

From behind him he heard the sound of a chair being pushed back and then a voice. It was a voice he hadn't heard for three years but it was a voice he instantly recognised. It was Baccary. "What the heck are you doing here in a place like this?" said Sam. The men embraced. Baccary explained that he was on his way to meet Sam and the road took him past the inn so he had decided to stop; one drink had led to another and he had drunk a little longer than he had planned, so decided to stay the night. However, Baccary did know who Sam was looking for, he had seen him earlier, and his name was Snowy White.

"But Sam," said Baccary, "what do you want with this man? I've come across men like this before and they're no good, they are thieves and cut-throats, the lowest of the low, you couldn't trust him for a second."

"I know," said Sam, "but I need some people who don't mind taking a risk and will do whatever I ask if the price is right."

"That's too risky, Sam, look at you, you're a respectable businessman, you can't be seen doing business with men like these."

"I need the monkeys gone, I thought I had explained that in my letter."

"Is there no other way?" said Baccary.

"No," said Sam. "I've considered everything, this is the only way. Do you know where he is?"

"He went out with the ebb tide early this morning

and won't be back until the tide's up tonight, and I'm sure he and his two scurvy crewmates have been up to no good."

"We'll wait," said Sam.

The two men settled to wait. They ordered more ale and a pork pie to eat while they waited.

"You know what," said Baccary as he looked at Sam, "you don't look a day older than you did the last time we met."

"People are always saying that," replied Sam. "Esme must be looking after me, married life suits me."

While they waited they talked about what had happened since they had last met. Sam explained how they had returned to England to stay and that he had bought a house in Tollesbury near his parents. His father-in-law Captain Brodie had retired and was now living in Wivenhoe and was a frequent visitor to Sam and his family. But where had Baccary been? Sam explained how he had tried to contact him on several occasions. Baccary spoke about how he had been living with his sister Effi and her husband and trying to set up overland trade routes with Europe. This had been incredibly difficult due to the political situation in the Gold Coast. Setting up any business was nothing but problems. However, he had found a reasonable overland route to trade and although trading was hard he had built up a small business. The biggest and best surprise was that Baccary had married and his wife was expecting their first child. For that reason Baccary was unable to stay for long. He told Sam that as soon as their business had been completed he would return home.

Just after nine that evening the shadow of Snowy White's boat, an old fishing smack called *Black Jack*, could be seen drifting with the flood tide up the creek. *Black Jack* was perfect for what Sam wanted. She was an old fishing smack about fifteen metres long with a big storage hold in the centre of the main deck and importantly she had a very shallow draft, which meant she could sail in the shallow waters of the salt marsh. The boat was soon moored up to the staging across the road from the inn. Sam and Baccary stood on the shore and waited. As soon as Snowy stepped ashore and set eyes on Sam he recognised him.

"You, you!" he shouted. "I know you, you're that piece of flotsam that led to the death of three of my best men." And with that he drew his sword and ran at the unarmed Sam. Baccary stepped in his way, threw him to the floor and held him there with his Mambele knife against his throat. Snowy's two crewmates jumped ashore and came towards Baccary.

"Stop right there, you dogs!" he shouted. "If you want your boss to still have breath, you stop right there." They stopped.

"Let's talk," said Sam. "Put your blades down and let's talk."

"OK, lads, do as he says," gasped Snowy reluctantly.

"Now, that's better. Tell your men to stay out of our way and let's you, me and Sam go into the inn and have a drink, we've got some business to discuss." Sam led the way into a small seating area hidden away from the main bar; Snowy and Baccary followed him.

Once seated Sam placed a small bag of gold sovereigns on the table and told Snowy what he wanted him to do. Sam explained how he had written to the newly opened London Zoo and offered them three African monkeys. He was purposely vague about what sort of monkeys they were and to be honest he wasn't absolutely sure. As far as he was concerned they came from Africa and were about the size of a small human and had green fur on their backs. What he didn't tell them was what incredible strength they had and how wild they could be when their fiery red eyes lit up. The zoo had responded to say they would be delighted to house the monkeys in a secure enclosure. They went on to say that they had been trying to enlarge their collection and were especially keen to have a family of monkeys. Since they had opened to the public monkeys had always been a very popular attraction. Sam knew this all too well as it had been his idea all those years ago when he brought the monkeys to England.

"You and I have both seen what those creatures can do," said Snowy. "They have been terrorising this salt marsh ever since you brought the furry green monsters here and now you want me to put it right, and you think a couple of gold sovereigns is going to buy me? I spit on you, my friend, and I curse you for what you have done."

"Only you and I know the truth about the monkeys and you must see the best place for them is in a secure enclosure at the zoo, and don't forget your men attacked me! I'll be with you, we just need to sail them down into the River Thames and London," said Sam. "And I have a plan. We shall place a false floor over the hold on the *Black Jack* then bring your boat to where the Greenbacks' nest is located. I know the spot. I will attract their attention, they'll recognise me. I will be their bait. As they come across the false floor to the hold to get me, you and your men will spring the trap and collapse the floor and drop the monkeys into the hold whereupon the hatch covers will be bolted down, holding then captive. Once in the hold they will be no problem and the trip into London is straightforward sailing. With a fair tide we will be there and back in less than thirty-six hours."

"How much you going to pay?"

"Fifty guineas, and that is more than you and your men would earn in a year," said Sam.

Snowy laughed and got up to leave. Baccary took hold of his arm and forced him to sit.

"Fifty for you and ten for each of your men," said Sam.

"One hundred and I'll sort out my men," replied Snowy.

"Very well," said Sam. "Keep the sovereigns and the rest you will get when the monkeys are in London."

"No," said Snowy. "My men and I are not risking our lives before we have the money."

"You'll get the rest of the money when the monkeys are secured in the hold of *Black Jack* and not before," replied Sam.

The deal was done. Sam was slightly relieved and

pleased as he was prepared to go as high as one hundred and fifty. It was agreed the men would all meet again at nightfall the following evening. Sam, Baccary, Snowy and his three men.

Just before the men parted company Baccary grabbed Snowy by his neck and said slowly and purposefully, "Don't you tell a soul and if you mess this up I'll come looking for you. You won't know where or when, but I will come looking for you." Snowy slunk away into the darkness.

Sam and Baccary rode back along the sea wall path in Sam's carriage, careful not to awaken any sleeping Greenback. Baccary expressed his concerns. Over the years he had met many men like Snowy and he had never met one he trusted.

"You worry too much," said Sam. "Just remember, not a word to Esme. She must never know what we plan to do."

It was a real surprise when Esme and the children woke the following morning to find Baccary sitting in their kitchen. They had only met him on three previous occasions and each time the saddest day was when he left. Baccary had almost achieved some sort of celebratory status in the village as men of colour were seldom seen, if ever in that part of the country.

Some remembered him from years ago when he had arrived back with Sam and Tommy. As he walked down the high street he was warmly welcomed back as an old friend visiting. However, there was no time to lose. Later that day Sam and Baccary made the excuse to leave; they told Esme not to wait up as they were going for a drink in the village followed by a bit of late-night fishing on Sam's small boat. "Just be careful," said Esme, and the men left.

Sam and Baccary arrived at where the *Black Jack* was moored. There was no sign of Snowy or his men. "I don't like this," said Baccary. "Where are they?"

"They'll be here soon enough," said Sam. And they waited. Thirty minutes later Snowy and his men turned up. "Where have you been? You're late," said Sam.

"We're here now, let's get on," replied Snowy with a sly grin. They boarded the boat.

Baccary pulled Sam aside. "They're all drunk, the idiots, they'll get us all killed."

Sam had recognised this himself.

"You shouldn't have given them those sovereigns last night, I told you not to. It's not safe, Sam, let's leave it and go home."

"No," said Sam, "there's no going back, I want this done and I want it done tonight. My contact at the zoo is expecting us." They cast off and the *Black Jack* drifted out into the creek. Sam knew exactly where to go and exactly how he was going to get to the Greenbacks.

It was two hours before high water. Sam instructed the crew to release the anchor at the back of the boat and then run the boat up onto the salt marsh until she grounded on the mud. The anchor would be used to pull the boat out of the marsh and into deep water once the monkeys were secured onboard and the tide had risen enough for the boat to float off.

The boat ground to a halt on the mud leaving a two-metre gap between the boat and the land. The rowing boat that was kept on the old smack's deck was lowered into the water and placed in position to bridge the gap between the smack and the land. Sam made one last check to reassure himself that the trap would work; his life would depend on it. He spoke to the crew to make sure they knew exactly what to do, then he went to step ashore. Baccary stopped him and urged him not to go. "I just don't trust them," he said. "They're all drunk, can't you see that?"

"Don't worry about them, we just need to get the

Greenbacks secured in the hold. You just make sure that trap is sprung or I'm a dead man." And with that, Sam stepped ashore.

It was a clear night and Sam was thankful for the light of the moon. Carefully he worked his way to where he had last seen the monkeys' den, making sure that he knew exactly what his route back to the *Black Jack* would be because when it came to the time to go back, he would have to go back very quickly. He got as close to their den as he dared, paused and then threw two small explosive devices, designed to make more noise than damage, towards the monkeys. They worked as intended and the monkeys jumped to their feet; as they did, Sam shouted at them to gain their attention. Spotting Sam, the Greenbacks launched themselves towards him. He turned and ran, screaming at the top of his voice, "We're coming! Get ready!"

As Sam reached the *Black Jack* he noticed that the rising tide had caused the gap between the land, the rowing boat and fishing smack to widen but there was no stopping now. Sam made one big jump onto the rowing boat then another onto *Black Jack*, grabbing at the rigging to help him swing himself aboard. The monkeys were much more nimble and were on board a split second behind him. Sam threw himself across the false hatch cover, shouting at Baccary, "Now! Now!"

Baccary pulled the rope, causing the hatch covers to collapse into the hold complete with three monkeys and Sam. As the covers fell Sam stretched out his arms and grasped the edge of the hold to stop himself falling any further. He ended up with his legs and body dangling above the three monkeys who were lying in a dazed heap on the floor beneath him. As Baccary helped pull him to safety the crew quickly fastened the hatch covers in place, containing the captured monkeys below. The plan had worked.

The anchor was hauled in, pulling the *Black Jack* out into deep water; the rowing boat was left in the water and put in tow astern and they were off. But things seldom are that simple, especially when you're working with a group of men who appear to be more interested in drinking bottles of rum. The crew were becoming more rowdy, shouting, singing and fighting amongst themselves, pleased with their evening's work, but that wasn't the worst concern, it was when they stopped being rowdy and started to whisper that Baccary and Sam became worried. Then Baccary realised what he had most feared was becoming reality, he had seen the signs before. Snowy and his three crewmen approached them. Snowy was displaying his menacing toothless smile that Sam had first seen on Hall Lane all those years ago. "We've had a change of plan," he said. And he drew an old revolver from the belt around his waist and pointed it directly at Sam. "Now," he said, "you've got a choice. You can take your chances down below in the hold with the monkeys or you can choose to swim. What will it be?" His men closed in on Sam and Baccary.

"What do you mean?" said Sam. "What about the monkeys?"

"Don't you worry about those monkeys now, we'll deal with them creatures, they won't be bothering anyone again and we have a score to settle with them after what they did to my men all those years ago. Now make your choice, die with the monkeys or take your chances swimming."

Baccary felt for the Mambele knife in his belt.

"I wouldn't be doing that now," shouted Snowy. "You've got to the count of ten. One, two..."

Sam interrupted his counting. "I'm surprised you can count, you illiterate sea dog," he growled as he moved to the starboard side of the boat. As he did so, the eyes of his assailants followed him and in that split second while he was not seen Baccary withdrew his Mambele. With one swipe of his knife he was able to disarm Snowy and push him back along the narrow deck into his crew. Sam took a dagger he was carrying concealed under his jacket and cut the ropes securing the hatch covers, releasing the monkeys. The two men then ran to the rear of the boat and jumped into the rowing boat that was being towed behind. With a final swipe of his trusty Mambele knife Baccary severed the rope that attached the small rowing boat to the *Black Jack* and they were free and away. Their backup plan had worked, they had escaped. The *Black Jack* disappeared out to sea with only the sound of fighting between the monkeys and Snowy's crew.

"Let's hope that's an end to it and the wind blows that boat so far out to sea she never returns," said Sam in a gravelly, low-pitched voice. Baccary didn't speak, he just nodded. He was never as optimistic as Sam.

They rowed back to the shore and returned home, happy in the knowledge that the monkeys apparently were gone. Maybe it hadn't gone completely to plan, but as Baccary had always said, always have a plan B and plan B had worked; they had done what they set out to do and that was to get rid of the monkeys. The boat was adrift and on its way out to sea.

But what had happened after they had left the *Black Jack*? What had happened to Snowy and his crew and the three Greenbacks they had left on *Black*

Jack? It was never Sam's intention for the monkeys to die, but he couldn't help feeling a sense of relief now that they were gone.

THE RETURN

Sam found himself unable to keep away from the Saltings. He didn't want to go down to the salt marsh; there was no need now the monkeys had gone, and he had no business there. But try as he might, he couldn't stop thinking about it. He needed to be sure, he just needed to take a quick look, just to make sure. He knew it would be a waste of time, but it would put his mind at ease knowing that the monkeys were gone. He could wait no longer; two days after he and Baccary had rowed away from the *Black Jack*, leaving Snowy and his crew to whatever fate awaited them, Sam returned to the Saltings. Sam went alone, it didn't take long, and as soon as he had climbed over the sea wall on a remote part of the marsh he could see it. Sam's worst fear had come true. In the distance he could see it on its own in the salt marsh, the unmistakable old fishing smack *Black*

Jack! All the hatch covers were missing, the sails were in rags and the boat was deserted.

As Sam drew closer he could see all the signs that there must have been a serious incident. The decks were streaked with what looked like blood, but whose blood was it? Sam couldn't be sure, was it the Greenbacks' or Snowy's? Either way, he was in big trouble. He quickly returned home and found Baccary in the forge with his father. It seemed to be his favourite place and Sam had often thought that Baccary would have been a better son to his father than he ever was or could be. He took Baccary to one side and told him what he had seen.

"We must go onto the marshes to see if they are back, we need to know. If they are we know that Snowy and his men will more than likely be dead. The problem is, if they are back they now know I'm here and if they are back they will come looking for me, and that's for sure."

The two men waited until early morning the next day. They knew exactly where to look and in his heart Sam knew what he would find. He found it; in their usual spot he could see them sitting in the marsh, three Greenback monkeys, two adults and one youngster, sitting as if nothing had happened. In less than three days this was the second time he had to resort to a new plan. Plan A to take the monkeys to the new zoo in London had failed; plan B, escaping from the *Black Jack* and Snowy's gang, leaving Snowy's gang and the monkeys drifting off out to sea to who knows where hadn't worked.

Sam turned to Baccary and said, "Plan C, we need a plan C."

"What?" exclaimed Baccary. "Plan C?" He sighed, looked up to the sky and turned to walk back to the village.

What was plan C? Plan C was to leave, leave Tollesbury and leave England. Sam couldn't stay, he couldn't risk the Greenbacks finding him and finding where he lived with Esme, Charlotte and George. He had to go and he had to go quickly. But what was he going to tell his family?

"Just stick to the plan," Baccary reminded him. "If we stick to the plan everything will be fine. But you must tell Esme now."

Sam told Esme and the children. He explained that there was a real business opportunity for him back in Bombay and that he and Baccary had to get there as soon as possible. She would be well provided for financially while he was away and if the business went well they would be financially secure for the rest of their lives. And then he lied, the first and only time he ever lied to Esme, he told her he would be back in less than a year. He would quickly conduct the business he needed to do then leave Baccary in charge while he returned to England. He did do the business as quickly as he could and he did leave Baccary in charge, but he was gone for two years.

Within twenty-four hours and after a very tearful farewell the two men had booked their passage and were gone. First stop was Accra. They would not be able to do anything until Baccary's wife had given birth to their first child. They stayed there for four months then once they were sure mother and baby were well they moved on to Bombay.

Over the following thirty years this became the established pattern. Every eighteen to twenty-four months Sam would come home, spend two or three months with his family, check to see if the monkeys were still there and then return to India. What Sam couldn't believe was that the monkeys were still alive. He had calculated that the older ones must be over forty years old. His research told him that there was no known record of any monkeys living to that age in the wild. His hope that they would pass away from natural causes and his life could return to normal was becoming more unlikely. He missed Esme and the children every minute he was away and although he had always loved the sea, the trip between India and England was becoming tedious.

The office in Bombay was working really well; they had recruited a group of very loyal and able staff who were all Indian nationals. Sam was keen to employ a local workforce – he believed in supporting the local community. He also believed that if he was loyal to them and respected them they would serve him well. And they did.

After ten years the business had become well established, trading cotton and silk. Then one day Baccary entered the office and said, "We need to expand the business. I've been talking to my sister Effi and she has told me that since you British had taken control over the Gold Coast there were possibilities for developing our business, especially by trading in cacao." Cacao is an essential ingredient when producing chocolate and at that moment in time Victorian England couldn't get enough of it. And as Baccary pointed out, Accra was only a six-week journey from England. Not being a couple of men to hesitate, by the end of that week they were on their way to Accra, leaving the Bombay office in the capable hands of a local man who had started with the company the day they arrived and was now appointed as their new junior partner.

And so it was, a new trading office was established in Accra and Sam continued his commuting between Accra and Tollesbury. For twenty years Sam split his time between two homes. The business was a success, he was able to provide his family with everything they wanted except his time, the thought that the monkeys would find him and his family was his constant fear. Life was good; Charlotte went on to do what her mother had always wanted to do and studied medicine at the Elizabeth Garrett Anderson Hospital in London. It must have been their mother's influence, for both Charlotte and George trained as doctors. Sam was proud of both of them.

*

Harry had been listening to Sam telling the story for almost two hours when Sam suddenly stopped.

"Is that it?" asked Harry. "What happened next?"

There was a long pause before Sam spoke again. Then he said, "Listen carefully, Harry, for if I continue I'm going to be telling you things you may find hard to believe, you may not want to believe, but once said cannot be unsaid. We can stop now, you can go back to your own bed and return home in the morning. If I continue you may find that your life will never be the same again."

Harry was confused; he wasn't sure what Sam meant. "How is this going to affect me?" he asked. "I can't even see how it has anything to do with my father."

"I haven't finished yet," said Sam. "You best leave, it's been a pleasure meeting you." And with that, Sam stood up and offered Harry his hand.

Harry didn't move, he was deep in thought. Then he said, "Hang on a minute, you can't stop there. You have not spent the last two hours telling me this story just to end it there. There is something you want from me. What is it, old man? Finish your story and we shall see what we shall see. And it's not even midnight and there is still half a bottle of whiskey waiting to be finished, unless you're saving that for a Greenback monkey." He laughed. Sam did not.

Sam poured them both another glass of whiskey and continued the story, but before he started he said, "Harry, whatever you hear tonight you must promise whether you believe it or not, you will never ever tell anyone and that whatever you think once I've told you, you must know that I have always done what I believed to be the right thing."

Harry sipped at his whiskey. "Tell your story," he

said. "I want to know what happened to your namesake."

Sam continued…

In all the visits Sam made back to Tollesbury one thing was becoming clear to all those who knew him, he remained very young looking and never seemed to get any older. Sam had noticed it too. He also noticed that every time he saw the Greenback monkeys they too looked no older. Sam dismissed it from his mind; he had other things to think about. His daughter Charlotte had married a man called Earnest, he was a colleague of hers and also a doctor. Their first child had just been born, a baby boy. And Sam's son George had decided to move to Accra. From an early age George had always said he wanted to practice medicine in Africa, so two years after completing his training he left home to work in a town thirty miles inland from Accra. It had been something that Baccary had arranged and he had promised Sam and Esme he would keep an eye on him.

Everything with the children was fine, but it was Esme who caused him concern. She was unwell. She had not been well for some time. Sam had had several doctors to see her but the prognosis was not good.

Sam could see for himself that things were bleak to say the least. There was no cure. For the final days of her life he sat with her day and night. She was the love of his life, the mother of their wonderful children, and also, it turned out, more knowledgeable about what was happening in Sam's life than he thought, despite his efforts to keep it secret. As he sat with her on her dying bed she told him that she knew all about the monkeys on the salt marsh, how they had got there and why he had to go away to keep the family safe. Baccary had told her. She had understood why Baccary had told her and she had promised to never let on to Sam that she knew. She told Sam how thankful she was for Baccary and what a good friend he had become to the family.

Sam thought about the first time he and Baccary had met outside St Albans all those years ago. He wondered what ever had happened to Tommy, Baccary's monkey. Next time he saw Baccary he would ask him. He hoped he could remember, Baccary was an old man now, but still as strong as an ox. Then Esme told him what he knew but didn't believe. She told him what he had long suspected himself; he was cursed. Baccary had told her. He had spoken to some of the elders from the village near where they trapped the Greenbacks. He had explained that his friend who had trapped the monkeys never seemed to age and the monkeys were still alive. They weren't certain, but two of the elders remembered an old story that if you crossed a Greenback they could curse you. Had they cursed Sam? Was it a curse to live forever, never growing old? Certainly Sam was not aging as you would expect; he was starting to look a bit older for sure, but he wasn't ageing like other men of his age. Baccary wasn't sure, but he was sure something strange was going on so he told Esme. They had decided not to tell Sam, but now on her dying bed she had decided to tell him. "Sam," she said, "you have been cursed, cursed to live forever, and it is a curse, Sam, and it comes from those monkeys who are cursed with you. You and they will never die until they are returned to where they come from. You must return them, Sam, you must return them."

That was her dying wish; she passed away later that evening. Sam was completely heartbroken. How could he carry on without Esme?

He had to fulfil her last wish and then in death he could join her again. Sam had to return the Greenback to the clearing in the jungle where they were trapped and lift the curse.

But how would he do it? He was grief stricken, how could he carry on living without Esme? He was scared, he was a broken man, broken with grief and he did what he always did in those situations, he ran away. He ran as far as he could, back to India and into the Himalayan Mountains. He was not seen again for thirty years.

Harry stopped him. "How do you know? That's a ridiculous story."

Sam put down his glass, looked Harry in the eye and slowly and purposefully said, "Surely you must have guessed by now. I am Sam Shine, son of a blacksmith from Tollesbury, husband of Esme and by my reckoning about one hundred and fifty years old." Nobody moved and nobody spoke.

Then Harry said, "That's rubbish, you are making this up. Yes, I've heard the stories about the mysterious marsh monkeys, but nobody believes that."

Over the many years that the monkeys had lived on the salt marshes, they had adapted themselves well to the environment. They had learnt to hide deep in the marsh where people seldom go, parts of the marsh that are often cut off by the high tide. During the day they stayed hidden, preferring only to move at night.

"Your father knew they were there," said Sam.

"How did you know my father? I'm sure he wouldn't have believed your crazy story," replied Harry, surprised that his father might be involved with this crazy old man.

"Really?" said Sam. "What do you think he built this boat for? Why do you think he had the reinforced forward cabin made?"

It was true, thought Harry. Why did he have this boat built with that special cabin? "How did you meet him and why was he going to help you?" he asked Sam.

"Think," said Sam. "Think about your family history."

Harry thought back. His father, Peter, had recently died and Sam obviously knew him, did he know his mother? "What was my mother's name?" he asked Sam.

"Is that really the most challenging question you can ask me?" said Sam. "Her name was Joan, Joan Wilson, and then she married your dad and became Joan Wright. She was the daughter of a shipping agent and it was her father's firm that she and Peter eventually took over. And who were your grandparents?" he asked Harry.

Harry had very fond memories of his grandparents and the time he had spent with them. He paused for a minute to think; they were just Granny and Granddad to him, then he remembered and said, "Earnest Wright and Charlotte Wright."

"And what was Charlotte's maiden name?" asked Sam.

Harry thought then said, "I don't know, I can't remember."

"Can you remember her brother's name, your great uncle?" Sam asked.

"I'm not sure, but I do know he went abroad."

"Yes," said Sam, "he went off to Africa to work as a doctor, he met up with Baccary who supported him when he first arrived there, and Charlotte's maiden name was Shine, and she was my daughter and you are my great-grandson!"

Harry gasped. Could it be true or was he just a crazy old man? Was he his great-grandfather? Was this the man who Granny Charlotte wouldn't talk about, the man his mother had often referred to as being the mysterious friend who turned up unannounced to her displeasure? It did all seem to fit together. "Why had they only rarely spoken about you?" he asked.

"Nobody was proud of what I had done. Would you want to tell your children their grandfather was cursed and had brought that curse home to Tollesbury with three cursed monkeys and just left them there?" He paused, and then continued. "I have spent my whole extended life trying to put right what I have done wrong, I have provided for the family my whole life, none of you have wanted for anything. But still I am not free of the curse. Your father and your grandfather have both tried, now I am here with you."

"But where have you been? Where did you go?"

"I went away thirty years ago. After about fifteen years I returned briefly to see your grandparents to make sure everything was well. Your grandmother Charlotte was a kind and generous lady, she would beg me to stay longer, but once I had checked to see if the monkeys were still here I would leave. Every time I visited I would hope that after all the years that had passed the monkeys would have finally passed away, moved on or disappeared. I didn't really care, I just hoped that they would no longer be here, but it was never to be. Those were dark years and dark times."

The two men settled back down, poured another glass of whiskey and Sam continued with his story.

"I made four visits back to Tollesbury during that thirty-year period. As I said, I would always have a hope that the Greenbacks had gone, somewhere, anywhere. I made all sorts of plans of how I would rid the salt marshes of those Greenbacks, but the task was an almost impossible one for a single man and I was reluctant to ask for any help. Baccary was several years older than me and he wasn't cursed to live forever. He had developed the business well in Accra and had a lovely family, I couldn't ask him to leave them. Although I knew if I had asked, he would not have hesitated in stopping whatever he was doing and would have followed me wherever I was going. He was a good friend. For that reason I knew I could never have asked him. He did return to Tollesbury once with me, much to Charlotte's delight. They really did have a soft spot for each other. We had a marvellous two weeks, the memory of which has stayed with me as fresh as if it was yesterday. I never saw him again. Soon after his return to Accra he passed away peacefully in his own home with his wife and children by his side. I have kept in contact with his family and have visited them often, but I miss him almost as much as I have missed Esme."

Harry interrupted Sam. "I heard several stories about the monkeys over the years, most of them I don't believe, but there were two that stick in my mind. I have always dismissed them as groundless, made-up stories, maybe enhanced over time. The first involved a crash landing of a German bomber in 1940 and the fate of its crew and the second involved a Thames sailing barge that was used as an outdoor adventure centre for children from London. They always seemed a bit far-fetched to me."

"Things are never as they may seem," said Sam. "I was there on both occasions and I'll tell you what happened. On the first occasion you mentioned I had returned home to meet up with your father. And I can tell you now the whole event had absolutely nothing to do with the Greenback monkeys. Your father and I were on this very boat, the *Sandpiper*. She was almost new then. It was the first time I really had a chance to talk to him. He was a real old-school adventurer and nothing was going to stop him in helping me, that's for sure."

"That's just like him, the bit Mum wasn't so keen on. But it did make him the man he was and the man I don't want to be like," said Harry.

Sam continued, "Well, we were onboard *Sandpiper* talking about how we were going to rid the marshes of the monkeys. The Second World War was well underway and bombing raids on London and many other cities were regularly taking place. That night at about eight p.m. we suddenly heard the sound of bombs exploding in the distance. We knew it couldn't be London, that's too far away for us to hear, so we guessed they must be bombing Harwich or Felixstowe. However, we didn't pay too much attention to them as it seemed extremely unlikely that anyone would want to drop bombs on the salt marsh at Tollesbury. It all went quiet and we thought the raid was over, and then we heard it, a lone aircraft. As the noise became louder we realised it was coming our way. We went out on deck and we could see it in the distance. It was a twin-engined plane, but one of the engines had a trail of flames and smoke bellowing from it. As it approached it was getting lower and lower. It wasn't long before we realised it was going to crash.

"The pilot flew low over the salt marsh and clearly recognised the marsh as a good option for making a crash landing. He overflew the marsh, banked round to starboard and came in low to land. It surprised us as it was not a German plane, it was an Italian Fiat BR20 belonging to the Italian air force. The pilot was truly exceptional; he kept the landing gear fully retracted and brought the plane down perfectly, bouncing along the marsh and coming to a halt fifty metres in front of the *Sandpiper*. Your father and I ran through the mud to pull the crew clear. Just as we did, the plane burst into flames we were too late. The crew were stuck in the wreckage; they didn't have a chance despite the best efforts of the pilot.

"In the distance we could see local men from the village armed with whatever they could find running towards the wreckage. Then we saw him, a young airman who had obviously been thrown from the aircraft as it crash landed. He was lying covered in blood and mud ten metres from the *Sandpiper*. He was unharmed apart from some bruising and minor cuts, but was clearly confused and very, very frightened. We brought him aboard *Sandpiper*, your father, me and an Italian airman. He spoke very little English and was in shock, we had no idea what to do with him. Shortly after we could hear the group of men from the village arrive. They looked so angry that we were worried they might do something to the young airman that they may later regret, so we kept him hidden. The flames from the fire raged on and the men were looking for bodies. They must have got fed up with searching because one of the men started shouting. 'The Greenbacks have got them, it's the Greenbacks!" they shouted. We said nothing. The locals kept going on about the Greenbacks so we let them continue to believe that. Some of the men started searching the surrounding area, but as the fire died the men drifted off back to their homes and we were left with one very young, scared Italian airman.

"The plane had taken off from an airfield in Belgium earlier that evening to bomb Harwich and to this day I don't know if we did the right thing or whose idea it was. But we took him back to Belgium. It was just after 10pm and the tide was high when we slipped out of the creek and sailed overnight. It was a twenty-hour trip to the coast of Belgium; the most worrying part was when it was daylight and we were in the middle of the North Sea. As darkness fell we closed in on the Belgian coast. It was far too risky to land so we made the decision to put the Italian into a lifejacket and let him swim ashore. He was more than happy to do so. We said goodbye and sent him on his way. He thanked us profusely, jumped over the side and was gone. We turned the boat about and headed for home. However, some years later we received a letter, it was from the young airman thanking us for our kindness and enclosing a photo of his young family. The photo was taken on the steps of a church in a village outside Naples. He was the minister of that church. It made me think of my grandfather.

"We arrived back to Tollesbury the following evening. It had been two days since the plane crashed but it had significantly interrupted our plans as your father was due to report for duty on board his navy minesweeper at Harwich at the end of the week, and this meant we didn't have enough time for our plan to catch the monkeys. The war was on and your father had gone to do his duty, so I left. I took the *Sandpiper* to the only safe place I could think of, Ghana, and Baccary's family. Baccary had died years earlier, but I still kept in contact with his family. They understood what was happening, they knew about the curse and they always welcomed me like I was returning home. I stayed there for some time. When the war was over I did make a quick visit, just to check, hoping again that the monkeys were gone, but knowing deep inside they couldn't be. They weren't.

"Your father was getting married, and Charlotte was quite elderly so I decided the time was not right to catch monkeys, so soon after the wedding I left.

"Now the incident with the Thames sailing barge you mentioned, that was everything to do with the Greenbacks. It was early in October, your father and I had a new idea which we had been planning for some time. Your father was arranging for a special boat to be built, a boat big enough and with a cabin strong enough to keep the monkeys safe while we sailed them back to Africa. Had you never wondered about why your father's boat was designed the way it was and why that forward cabin was left bare and the door reinforced?"

Harry had pondered on this for some years. Every time he asked his father he received some sort of fudged answer and the topic of conversation was quickly changed. And to be really honest Harry didn't care much for boats anyway, so he didn't want to appear too interested in case his father would ask him out on a trip.

Sam went on. "So again, we were sitting aboard *Sandpiper* discussing ways of loading the Greenbacks onto his boat once we had trapped them. While we were passing the time on my boat, one hundred yards down the creek was an old Thames sailing barge. It was used as an outdoor education centre for children from London. I thought it was a really good thing but couldn't really understand the need. When I was a youngster I had all the outdoor play I needed and it generally got me into trouble. However, they seemed to be having fun. The barge had been cleverly converted down below to provide a number of small cabins for the children to sleep in. Every cabin had had a porthole fitted, a non-standard feature for a Thames barge, they didn't have portholes as their main use was to carry cargo. Every night the children were given clear instructions – make sure your porthole is closed and locked before you go to sleep – and every night one of the leaders on board would go into each cabin and check that the children had followed instructions and that the portholes were closed.

"Well, there were fifteen children onboard for a week's break, and as with most groups of people there is always one that finds following instructions difficult. In this case it was boy called Christopher; he was a bit of a loner and preferred his own company. His parents had insisted he go on the trip in the hope he would make some friends. He was friendly enough but preferred to keep himself to himself and seldom gave anyone any trouble, so much so that he was often forgotten about. What seems to have happened is that while everyone was out taking part in various fun activities he was doing something completely different. He was feeding and befriending a small monkey! It was by accident at first; his mother had packed his favourite snack, two big bags of peanuts. As the other children were playing he had wandered out onto the marsh were he sat himself down and started eating some nuts. In his clumsiness he dropped a handful. The nuts rolled down the embankment and out of reach. As he sat watching, a small hand appeared and scooped up the nuts. The young boy looked on with interest and threw a couple more nuts down, the hand appeared again. Again, he threw down more nuts and this time the hand appeared followed by a head and a body, the body of a small monkey. Just then, the whistle went, a sign that the children had to return to their base on the barge. As quickly as it had appeared, the monkey disappeared and the boy returned to the barge.

"The next day the boy returned to the same spot and threw down some more nuts, and as had happened the previous day a small monkey appeared again. By the third day the monkey came and sat next to the boy. That evening the boy was getting ready for bed when he looked out of his porthole and there, outside his porthole on a small island of mud and seaweed sat a small monkey. The boy was really pleased to see the monkey and shared his nuts again. It was his secret, he told nobody.

"On the fourth night as the boy was preparing for bed, he looked out and saw not just one monkey as he expected, but three. The small monkey he had befriended and two larger monkeys. They were all similar in appearance. They were mostly covered with brown fur on their head, arms and legs, but on their back the fur turned to green from their bottom to their neck and on their chest was a bright patch of white fur. He was excited to see them all, and they were obviously excited to see him and to taste his peanuts, a favourite food for monkeys but as you can imagine, extremely rare on the salt marsh. The taste of the nuts caused quite a bit of excitement amongst the group of Greenback monkeys and they became quite noisy. The commotion the monkeys were making was heard by two other children on the barge who immediately went out onto the deck to see what was happening and to their surprise, they were confronted by a group of monkeys playing in the barge's rigging. The children just stopped and stared, and then started to scream at the top of their voice, 'Monkeys! Monkeys on board!'

"On hearing there were monkeys on board the other children below streamed out onto the deck, scrambling to get through the cabin door to see them. After that, a sort of panic broke out. The children were shrieking as they came on deck and the adult leaders were shouting at the children to be calm and in the panic an oil lamp was knocked out of its gimbals, spilling burning oil onto the cabin floor and the barge started to burn. The fire spread quickly below deck and smoke spilled out of the open doorway and portholes, adding to the panic and confusion. Most of the children had seen nothing as the elusive monkeys quickly disappeared.

"While all this was developing I was sitting on *Sandpiper* with your father. We had attempted to trap the monkeys the week before but had failed. Trapping monkeys on a salt marsh had proved to be incredibly difficult over the years. I had tried many different ways of catching them with your grandfather and father and I was becoming increasingly desperate to rid the marshes of this menace. As well as trapping I had tried drugging them and to my shame I had also contemplated drowning or shooting them. Our latest efforts had failed yet again; the soft muddy ground of the marshes had made it difficult to set the trap and the constant rain from the previous weeks had made it virtually impossible. The monkeys are so well camouflaged and had become so resourceful and clever that it was becoming more and more difficult to get anywhere near them, let alone catch them.

"Anyway, we suddenly started to hear all this commotion coming from the barge, the sound of voices shouting and children screaming. Like a flash your father was out of the cabin door. When he saw the flames and smoke he shouted for me to come quickly and to bring the fire extinguisher. We ran towards the barge; the tide was out and some of the children had ended up in the mud. This was just as well because if the tide was high they would have been washed out to sea. We helped the children and adults onto firm ground where we made sure everyone was safe and unharmed. Your father then took a fire extinguisher and went back on board the barge with one of the adult leaders to put out the fire. Luckily the fire was more smoke than flames and they were quickly able to bring it under control. When calm was restored and all the children accounted for the senior adult asked the children what they had seen. The children who had seen the monkeys spoke up. They said they had seen a group of monkeys in the rigging. Well, everyone turned to stare at the rigging; there was nothing there. 'Did anyone else see monkeys?' he asked. Nobody spoke. He turned to the two boys who said they had seen them and asked again, 'Are you sure? What did they look like?'

'"They were green and white. Two were quite big and one was small,' they answered.

'"Hmm,' said the senior leader as he turned to me and asked if I or your father had ever seen monkeys on the salt marsh. We both said no. I did expand on the answer, saying that there had always been a rumour that monkeys lived on the marshes but this had never been proven and that most people considered it to just a bit of old-fashioned folklore.

"Christopher, the child who had attracted the monkeys in the first place, said nothing, yet he was the only one that really knew. The children were taken to one of the old sail lofts in the village and in the morning they boarded a coach and were taken back to London. The old Thames sailing barge was left on the marsh where she lies today and nobody ever talks about monkeys, especially not green and white ones.

"After that I said goodbye to your father and went away again. I didn't think I would be away for that long, but when you're cursed to live forever the years slip by all too quickly and you forget that those who you love are getting older, and I was not. You return to places you have left some time before and because I hadn't changed I thought they wouldn't. I have had to face this true reality several times with great sadness, none more so than today when I returned to the salt marsh and thought that the first person I saw was my old best friend and grandson, Peter. And then to be told I was mistaken and that he and his wife had passed on to a better place. This has just been made worse by the fact that I only missed seeing him by a couple of months."

Sam stopped talking and Harry could see the sadness in his empty eyes. "I think that's enough for tonight," said Harry. "I'm going back to my boat, we'll talk again in the morning." With that, Harry and Sam said goodnight and Harry turned to leave. Just as he was about to exit the cabin door he turned to Sam again and said, "You will be here in the morning, won't you?" Sam didn't answer.

The Beginning of the End

Harry woke early the next morning and even before leaving his bunk he looked out of the window just to check and see if Sam was still there. He was; the *Sandpiper* was moored where he had left her just a few short hours earlier. All night he had tossed and turned, trying to decide what he should do. A small part of him was hoping that when he woke Sam would be gone and he would be able to return to his normal life working as a shipping agent and forget all about Greenback monkeys and his great-grandfather, but that was not to be.

What would his next step be? And did he really want to take it?

It was a bright and freezing cold morning in March. Harry was pleased, the last place he wanted to be was on the salt marsh on a wet, cold, miserable day. He'd done that more than once before with his father and had no memory of any of those days being particularly fun, although his father always loved the salt marsh no matter what the weather was doing.

He didn't bother with breakfast, just a mug of coffee before he went over to Sam's boat. It was the first time he had seen Sam's boat in broad daylight and his first impression was of an extremely well-made craft. He could see that only the very best materials had been used. The decks were laid with teak and the main structure was of the best Honduras mahogany. The quality of the craftsmanship in every element of the boat was clear to see, even though the boat was obviously very old and in places worn. Interestingly the two masts and all the rigging were in absolutely first-class condition along with all the deck fittings, a sure sign of belonging to someone who takes their sailing seriously and who is prepared for anything. Harry wondered how much it would cost to have a boat made of that quality today. He had some idea of what his father's boat was worth but Sam's was in a different league.

Harry knocked on the cabin door and waited to be invited in. His knock was answered almost immediately; he entered the cabin. Inside Sam was busy with diagrams on pieces of paper and charts spread out over the cabin table. Sam beckoned Harry in and indicated that he should sit next to where he was working. There was no greeting or small talk, Sam went straight to the topic of the day, catching Greenbacks. His hand-drawn charts of the salt marsh showed where the monkeys were based. On other sheets of paper he had diagrams of traps made up of ropes and nets. And on the wall in a cabinet on the main bulkhead of the boat there was a Winchester Model 70 hunting rifle. Harry knew nothing of rifles, he was just reading the label, but what he read didn't please him. "What's that for?" he asked.

"That is my last resort," said Sam. "I've had it for some time, but never used it. I've thought about it often, but I just can't bring myself to kill an animal. I have wondered whether or not it would work. Can they be killed by traditional methods like shooting? And if I was able to kill them what would happen to me? Would the curse be lifted, would I die? I just didn't know. However, coming back and finding your father had died was the last straw. I'm not going to mourn the death of any more of my closest friends and family. I've had enough. It must end now. I will do whatever it takes, shoot them or blow them up. I'm sure they couldn't survive a large explosion and if necessary I'll blow myself up with them, I've got nothing to lose. It has got to end now."

Harry could hear the desperation in Sam's voice. He stood up and walked to the cabin door to leave. "Where are you going?" asked Sam.

Harry told him, "I'm not staying with a desperate man who's holding a gun no matter what the circumstances are, even if he is my great-grandfather, and I'm not helping you to shoot monkeys. Goodbye."

"Wait!" cried Sam. "I can't do this without you, I need your help."

"Simple," said Harry. "Get rid of the gun and while you're at it you can get rid of that stupid knife with the curved blade that you keep tucked in your belt. There is no place for weapons such as those nowadays."

"But that's Baccary's Mambele throwing knife, I can't get rid of that," replied Sam.

"You wear that when you're off this boat and you will be arrested. Get rid of it," said Harry firmly.

Harry was clear; get rid of the gun and knife or he was not going to help. He also insisted that it was done right there right then, there was no way he was going to stay onboard his great-grandfather's boat while those weapons were still onboard.

"OK, what do you suggest?" said Sam. "Should I just throw it overboard here, now?"

"No," replied Harry. "Someone might find it. We need to take them out in the dinghy and dump them in deep water where nobody will find them and before we do that we should remove the firing pin and any other important part that makes it work."

"What, now?" said Sam.

"Yes, now," answered Harry.

Sam took the gun down from the bulkhead and did as Harry had asked. Under his breath Harry could hear Sam moaning something about how he was as stubborn as his father. The comment made Harry feel surprisingly good. They boarded the small dinghy that Sam had tied alongside *Sandpiper*. "Where's the engine?" asked Harry.

"There's nothing wrong with oars," replied Sam. And off they went. Sam rowing and Harry sitting on the rear bench seat with the now disarmed rifle next to him.

This is madness, thought Harry. *What am I doing? Twelve hours ago I was just a normal man. Now I'm sitting in a rowing boat watching a one-hundred-and-fifty-year-old man row me out into deep water so we can dump a high-powered hunting rifle and a Mambele throwing knife in a place no one will find them. I haven't even touched a rifle or for that matter a throwing knife in my life and I'm quite sure that I shall never want to. What next?*

He knew what was coming next, trapping monkeys, and he needed a plan. A better plan than what his great-grandfather had, because his plans hadn't worked. Harry knew, only a fool continues to do the same thing over and over again and expects a different result. He needed to think of something that hadn't been tried before.

They eventually reached a spot where the water was deep enough but still close enough to the shore to avoid being caught up in fishermen's nets. Without a word Harry threw the gun into the water then looked at Sam.

"Now the knife," said Harry.

Sam looked at him but could see there was nothing that was going to change his mind. He took the Mambele from his belt and uttered a few words in a language Harry didn't understand and threw the knife into the water. They rowed back in silence and within the hour they were back on board the *Sandpiper*. Harry was making coffee and Sam, still looking a bit put out and sulky, was preparing his plans. They sat and drank coffee as Sam told Harry of his plans in great detail.

How they would trap the monkeys, luring them one at a time. The monkeys had been too clever and elusive in previous attempts. Sam felt that if they could get the smallest one, which he thought would be the easiest to catch, they could use it as bait to catch the others, especially if they could put the small monkey in a life-threatening situation. He had planned to place the small animal in a cage on the marsh at low water. As the tide came in the monkey would drown, forcing the other two monkeys to attempt a rescue. It would be then when he would pounce, capturing them in a net. It would be a strong lightweight net that he would fire out of a sort of cannon, spreading out and covering the monkeys. Once captured they would be taken back to Sam's father's boat and placed in the specially reinforced forward cabin. Then they would be offered food which was laced with a sedative that would sedate them while he and Harry sailed them back to Africa.

Harry listened carefully and when Sam had finished, he asked how many times he had tried to trap the monkeys to date. Including the time he first caught them in the jungle, he answered that this would be his tenth attempt to catch them. All previous attempts except for the first one had ended in failure.

Harry could control himself no longer. With his left arm he swept everything off the table, even Sam's empty coffee mug. "You're mad," he said. "I can't believe my father went along with this madness. What is it they say? It's a sign of madness to do the same thing over and over again and expect a different result. We need to rethink this now before we go any further."

Sam was speechless. Nobody had suggested anything different in the past, and they had always looked to him for his ideas. He was at a loss to know what to do, he had no ideas, but maybe Harry was right, they had to try something different.

"First of all," said Harry, "we are not going to sail the monkeys back to Africa in my dad's old boat." The idea of sailing several thousand miles really didn't appeal to Harry. As a shipping agent he told Sam that he would have no problem getting them shipped back on one of the thousands of ships that visited Felixstowe docks each year. He identified two problems; the first was to get the monkeys onto the ship and the second was to get them off and back to where Sam had found them one hundred and twenty-five years ago in the clearing fifty miles inland from Accra, now the capital city of Ghana.

After several minutes contemplating what they had to do, Sam's eyes looked up. "Rose," he said. "We could contact Rose. She lives in Accra." Harry asked who Rose was and why she would help. "I'll write to her," said Sam. "I always write to her about once a year." Harry suggested he phone her. Sam looked bewildered, he hadn't thought of that, he didn't have a phone and had never considered getting one. Harry said he would phone her but Sam didn't have her number. Again, Harry asked who she was. Sam fetched a photo from a drawer in the cabinet by the cabin door. He showed the photo to Harry. "This is Rose," he said. "Your father was her godfather and she is Baccary's great-granddaughter."

Sam explained how Rose lived in Accra and managed the business Baccary's family had established years ago, exporting cocoa. Sam reassured Harry that she was very resourceful and would be an extremely useful contact. Harry took the smartphone from his pocket, Googled Rose's name and business, found a phone number but didn't call her, he didn't know what to say.

The two men sat for a while then went for a walk to the café in the old sail lofts. As they walked, they passed the hulk of the old Thames sailing barge deserted on the salt marsh. Harry looked at the wreck and a thought came into his head. "Remind me what happened on the boat," he asked Sam. Sam recounted the story about the boy feeding nuts to the monkey. "That's it," said Harry. "We need to feed them nuts." Sam wasn't convinced. "Listen," said Harry. "You've tried all the trapping and capturing ideas, you've even considered shooting them. Have you ever tried befriending them, gaining their trust? They just might be as keen to leave here and return to Africa as you are to get rid of them."

So as they ate breakfast at the café a new plan was discussed. It was different to anything Sam had tried before and it wasn't going to be a quick solution, it could take some time. Neither man had any experience of working with animals and gaining their trust. Neither of them had any idea of how long it would take. Would it be a month or a year? They didn't know. But they had to be ready and they needed the right equipment. They needed a really comfortable cage.

Back on the boat the men set about designing the cage. It would have to be no bigger than half standard size shipping containers which are normally forty feet long, nine feet wide and nine feet tall. Theirs would be twenty feet long. Three quarters of it would be open bars, but the final quarter would be enclosed to give the animals bedding and some privacy. One end would comprise of double doors and to the side at the rear there would be a smaller door to enable the cage to be cleaned out and fresh straw provided. It would be fitted to a trailer. They engaged a local firm of engineers based in the village to construct it.

Sam couldn't help but remember his father and his father's forge. Back in the day his father would have been more than capable of making it for them, but his father along with the forge were long gone, just a distant memory.

While it was being built Sam and Harry surveyed the marsh. They needed to find a spot where the cage could be positioned. If they were careful they would be able to tow the cage on its trailer behind a 4x4 along the service path which runs alongside the sea wall. They would then need a crane with a long-reach arm to lift the cage over the sea wall and position it on the edge of the Saltings. They would need to find somewhere where the ground was firm enough to take the weight of the vehicles and crane on the landward side of the wall, and also firm enough on the opposite salt marsh side to take the weight of the cage and high enough to keep it above the water when the tide was high. To help disguise the cage, they covered it with a sort of camouflage often used by the army, consisting of nets and green tarpaulins. Of course they had no idea how long it would have to be there.

"So who's going to feed nuts to the monkeys?" Sam asked.

Harry looked at Sam. "Have you got any other plans or somewhere you need to be? I've got a job to go to and after all, who brought them here?"

"What, every day?" said Sam.

"Every day, same time, come rain or shine for however long it takes. You've got to gain their trust and going by your record over the years that may take some time. Let's hope that the incident with the *Black Jack* and Snowy White is long forgotten."

It took two weeks to get the cage built and another week to get it into the right position. It was in a remote area near to where Sam believed the monkeys were. Not a place where people went very often, only the occasional hikers on the sea wall path. The old inn on Hall Lane had gone a long time ago along with the smugglers and vagabonds who used to frequent the place. All that was left now was Hall Farm. It was a very quiet area.

It did take some time. Every morning Sam left his boat and walked out onto the Saltings to the same spot at the same time seven days a week. It reminded him of the time he had first trapped the Greenbacks and how he had sat day after day waiting for them to appear in the clearing. His mind turned to the local guides who had deserted him there in the jungle and what had become of them. He remembered the heat of the jungle and the humidity. He wouldn't have minded a bit more heat in Tollesbury – it was April and it was wet; most days it rained. After two weeks there was still no sight of a monkey. Sam had to change his plan. He remembered what Harry had said, only a fool continues to do the same thing and expect different results.

Up until then he had only been on the Saltings during the day. So he decided that he would try to stay out on the marsh all night. After all, that was the time when most sightings had taken place. He would leave his boat at about eight o'clock each evening and not return until eight o'clock in the morning, then sleep during the day and return to his spot on the Saltings early evening. It was often wet and cold, but he persisted. After all, he didn't have anything better to do. Two weeks soon became three weeks, then a month. The weather was becoming warmer as they entered the month of May and Sam was starting to relax and enjoy the salt marsh. He started to notice the natural world of the Saltings he had never noticed before. The occasional wading birds that appeared as the sun rose in the morning and the splash of the mullet who circled round in the water as the tide flowed in. He even spotted two seals that had swum up the creek early one morning chasing fish.

It was towards the end of May that the first monkey appeared; the smallest and the most inquisitive. For days and nights Sam had been leaving nuts in a small pile near to where he was sitting. He left the pile of nuts when he returned to his boat and when he came back the nuts were there, untouched, just where he had left them. Then one day he returned to find them gone. He couldn't be sure it was monkeys that had taken them at first. Could it be birds or were there other animals running wild on the Saltings? He needed to be sure.

This went on for several days with Sam spending longer and longer on the marsh until finally, he was there all day and night, only returning to his boat to fetch more food. Of course Harry had been assigned the job of ensuring Sam had enough food to enable him to stay out on the salt marsh. Every couple of days Harry could be seen walking down the path towards Sam's boat with carrier bags of food.

Every other day he would ask the same question. "Any sightings yet?"

And always the answer had been the same. "No!"

But when he saw Sam on this day the answer was different. Sam could hardly contain his excitement. "I've seen him, I've seen him," he repeated. "He was there on the salt marsh no more than five yards away. I can't stop, I've got to get back." And with that, Sam said no more; he took the food from Harry and disappeared back onto the Saltings leaving Harry standing speechless.

His efforts had paid off. There he was, a small monkey taking his nuts. All he needed to do now was gain his trust. Well, if anyone has tried feeding a bird by hand you will know how difficult that can be. Each day Sam would put fewer nuts on the floor and when the monkey appeared he would sit perfectly still and hold out his hand full of nuts to the monkey. By the end of June that one monkey was eating out of his hand. By the end of July it was jumping and playing around him. His mind drifted back to when he had first found them and what fun they had been, and how he had enjoyed watching them play and how happy he was, and then how it had all changed in a blink of the eye. But he needed to gain the trust of all three monkeys. How long would he have to wait to find them?

He needed another plan. He had only seen and heard the other two Greenbacks on very rare occasions; neither of them had come anywhere near him. He would have to go to them. So one night he decided he would follow the small one home. If the others could see how friendly he was and how the little monkey trusted him they may also grow to trust him. He followed the little monkey back into the middle of the salt marsh where in the distance he could see the other two sitting peacefully. He didn't dare go too close.

The two monkeys suddenly turned and spotted him. Alarmed, they immediately jumped to their feet. Sam didn't move; he froze and sat perfectly still, hardly daring to breathe, holding out his hand full of nuts. He kept his gaze down, avoiding any eye contact and confrontation. It went quiet; neither he nor the monkeys moved. Did they know who he was? Maybe they too felt the need to finish this and go home and this might be their chance; he needed them to trust him. It was like time was standing still. Then the little one climbed up beside Sam and took a handful of nuts. He then took another handful and scrambled back over to where the other two stood and offered the nuts to them. They took them. It was the start of the next phase of gaining the monkeys' confidence.

Every day Sam would go to where the monkeys lived; he did not initially enter their space, he just sat nearby and held out a handful of nuts. The little one would come and play and carry nuts to the others who ate them happily. He had to move closer, but he didn't want to scare them. Gradually, day after day, he moved a little bit closer than he had been the previous day. And then he was there, in the centre of their camp feeding them nuts; all three Greenback monkeys were happily taking nuts from his hand. What a joy it was to Sam to see them so close up as he had remembered them. What handsome creatures they were. Part of him wanted nothing to change. Part of him wondered if he could just leave them on the Saltings forever, and then he would remember the curse and how he was cursed with them to live forever, and his only chance to free himself was to return the Greenbacks to where he had found them. But to do that he needed to move to the next stage of the plan, he needed to get them to come to him. To do this he again used the smallest monkey to help him. He would walk away from where the monkeys lived to where he was based by the cage, dropping a trail of nuts as he went. Back at the cage Harry had left a supply of different fruits. Sam offered the fruits one at a time to the small animal; it was important for Sam to find the one that the monkeys liked best. It was as he predicted, bananas. The monkeys had not seen or tasted a banana since before that fateful day all those years ago when Snowy White's gang had ambushed them. Going by the reaction he got to the bananas from the small monkey he was sure his plan would work.

Every day he would slowly walk to where the monkeys lived and offer them nuts; he never took bananas or any other fruit with him, he kept that back at the cage and only gave it to the little Greenback when he visited the cage. It wasn't long before the whole family were visiting him. By the end of August, Sam was actually sitting in the cage with the Greenbacks sitting and playing beside him. He wondered how he had been so frightened of them. Then he remembered Snowy White and his gang and what the Greenbacks were capable of.

In their peaceful mood they loved to swing from the ropes attached to the bars in the roof and to sit up on the wooden beams placed towards the top of the cage which was ten feet high. This was a skill they hadn't used for years; there are no trees on the Saltings. But these skills returned quickly. Sam sat and marvelled at the way they could swing from one side of the cage to the other, the way they carefully and skillfully peeled bananas, how they would play with him, taking his hat and passing it between them, placing it on each other's head in turn and when he wasn't looking they would take his water bottle and drink. It made Sam remember how it all started and that day near St Albans that he first met Baccary and his pet monkey Tommy. Could he keep them, he thought? Could he take them back home? But his home was a boat moored on the Saltings – that would never work. Could he take them back to Harry's house? It was only a fleeting thought; he knew what he needed to do, they deserved to go back home, he should never have stolen them in the first place.

He needed to start the next part of his plan, to close the door to the cage with the monkeys in it, something he had not done so far, he had always left the door open for them to come and go as they pleased. He knew he would only be able to do that once; if it went wrong and they escaped it would take forever to gain their trust again. He spoke to Harry to ensure everything was in place. The crane had been booked to lift the cage onto the trailer, a place for the cage had been reserved on a small cargo ship that was leaving Harwich for Ghana at the end of the following week and Rose had been contacted in Ghana and had said she would be ready with a Land Rover to tow the trailer when they arrived. The part of the plan that they were most concerned about was talking to Rose. Harry had never met her and had never talked to her before. Sam, who had met her and appeared to have a good knowledge of her, was not concerned at all.

When Harry phoned her, he explained who he was and what their plan was. He was surprised; Rose knew exactly who he was, who his father was – who she said she had met on several occasions – and then went on to say that his father, Peter, he had been her godfather. Harry once again felt hurt that his father had excluded him from this part of his life; he had never mentioned any of this to Harry, it was like he had a second secret life that nobody at home ever knew about. She even knew all about Sam Shine, her great-grandfather's best and lifelong friend. Without a second's hesitation she agreed to meet them and would be ready for when they arrived. Harry was pleased, he knew immediately that she was a person who he could trust. Harry smiled to himself. Speaking to Rose was surprisingly easy; he did not always find speaking to people easy, especially women. Which was why he preferred to spend most of his time on his own, but with Rose he felt relaxed. Everything was in place as long as it didn't rain, as that would make the path too soft for the crane. If it rained the whole plan would be a disaster. It stayed dry.

The day arrived. Harry arranged to take time off work. He wasn't sure how long it was going to take but he had a feeling it was going to take a while. He left the business in the safe hands of the management team, saying he had urgent family business to attend to in Ghana. He would keep in contact and let them know within the next few weeks when he was going to return. In his head he couldn't help thinking, *If I return!* Was he being foolhardy? He just didn't know.

The crane was positioned ready to lift the cage onto the trailer; all that they needed to do now was lock the doors of the cage once all three Greenbacks were inside. Sam was concerned about how they would react to the doors being locked. Would they stay calm, would they panic, would they feel safe and secure? He wanted them to feel safe and secure. He decided he would stay with them to keep them calm. He would lock himself in the cage with them. Harry was shocked by this plan. "You're mad," he said. "They will rip you to pieces if they panic. There is no way you can travel with the monkeys."

Sam was adamant; there was no way he was not going to be in that cage. He needed to be there. His bond with the three Greenback monkeys was now so strong he knew he would never leave them, not a second time. The first time he left them all those years ago was a mistake he was not going to make again. His future was bound to theirs.

That evening the monkeys came to the cage as usual; Sam and Harry had prepared the cage with fresh straw and a plentiful supply of fruit. They wanted to make it as comfortable as possible. As the Greenbacks entered the cage, settled on the straw and ate the fruit that Harry had left earlier, Sam stood up and slowly walked over to the doors. His heart was beating fast, he was breathing heavily. Slowly and silently so as not to disturb the animals he pulled the doors closed, locked them and then walked back to the monkeys and sat down beside them. The monkeys barely noticed and carried on eating. However, the next stage was not going to be so easy. Harry hooked up the straps from the crane to the cage and then before lifting it onto the trailer, he covered the cage with tarpaulins, leaving only the top uncovered to provide some light. The monkeys stopped eating and looked at Sam; Sam remained calm. Everything had to be kept as calm as possible, the last thing he wanted to do was excite the monkeys. Finally Harry attached onto the outside of the cage a very old sign he had kept in his garage for years. He wasn't sure where it had come from but it was very old. The sign said:

Sam Shine

World Famous Showman

The lift onto the trailer was as expected. The cage jerked and swung in the air, not a lot, but enough to cause some distress in the monkeys. Sam positioned himself in the middle of the cage and beckoned the monkeys to his side. He had to stay calm. He distracted them with nuts and fruit. He huddled together with them and then it was done, the cage was on the trailer and secured. Harry knew to pause for a while to allow the animals to settle before he set off towards the docks. It was a slick operation. Throughout the journey to the docks Sam constantly spoke calmly to the animals, reassuring them that everything was alright, telling them that after so many years they were going home, back to the jungle of Ghana, back to where they belonged and should never have been taken from. He knew he had done right by staying with them.

Harry had organised things well. There was little delay in arriving at the docks and being lifted into the hold of the ship. Harry completed all formalities and paperwork and the job was done. By midnight the Greenbacks were fast asleep, comfortable on mounds of straw and hay. Sam felt that they probably hadn't been that comfortable since he had last been in a cage with them. Sam left them sleeping and crept out of the cage to find Harry. Harry was in a cabin on one of the upper decks. It was a basic cabin but it had everything you needed. Sam took some food and a large glass of whiskey that Harry had in the cabin but he didn't stay. He went back to the where the Greenback monkeys were sleeping. He would not leave them again, not until the time and place were right.

By first light the ship was well on its way. The whole trip was so much more comfortable and so much quicker than it had been all those years ago. The Bay of Biscay was crossed and before long they were passing by Madeira and then the Canary Isles. In what seemed like no time at all the light of the new Jamestown lighthouse was looming bright, guiding them towards Accra. Then clearly in the morning sun they could see the old Cape Coast Castle high on the cliffs above Accra. Built to house slaves hundreds of years ago, the British government had taken it over at the end of that abominable trade. It had been the place where several well-known pirates had been hung. Now it had been abandoned with just a small museum inside to remind people of its awful past.

The ship finally docked just after midday. As quickly and as efficiently as it had been loaded the trailer and cage was unloaded. And there she was, waiting with a Land Rover as she said she would be, on the quayside. The sight of her took Harry's breath away. He had spoken to her several times after that first call and every time they spoke their conversation had lasted longer and longer. He felt he knew her well. But now there she was, waving at him and looking more beautiful than he could ever have imagined. He shouted at Sam, "There she is, on the quay, there she is!" Sam was only half interested, he was more concerned with the monkeys and he was strangely starting to feel tired. His bones were aching; the spring he had always had in his step was no longer there. He dragged himself to his feet and exited the cage to greet Rose with a kiss and a hug. Harry just stood. Now as he was closer to Rose he could see the shine in her eyes, her long dark hair and dark skin. She was tall and slim, she was in his opinion stunning. He just stood and stared. Rose released herself from

Sam's grip and ran to Harry, threw her arms around him and kissed and hugged him like a long-lost friend; he felt embarrassed but responded in a similar way.

Before they were to start their journey into the jungle Rose had decided that they should rest for a day or two at her house with her family. Rose took them to her parents' home. It was the most magnificent property, built high up on the hills overlooking Accra and the ocean, set in its own grounds which had been landscaped into a wonderful fertile garden. Her father was Baccary's grandchild and the family had all met Sam before; they welcomed both men with open arms and treated them as you would treat any member of your family that you hadn't seen for a long time.

The two days they spent there were glorious, the family couldn't do enough for them. Harry spent most of his time with Rose. They took long walks and drives into the town and jungle as Rose showed Harry the sights of Ghana. They chatted and laughed a lot. Sam spent most of his time with the Greenbacks. Rose's family had made a large enclosure for them where they could play and exercise after their long journey. They seemed happy, sensing they were nearing home again. Sam was not recovering well from the sea journey. His body ached more than it had before and he was feeling quite tired and frail. On the third day, early in the morning Sam led the monkeys back into the cage and locked the door. Harry and Rose hooked up the trailer and cage to the Land Rover and they left. It was a fifty-mile drive; it had taken Sam days to travel that distance years ago with his old wagon and his horse Bess. He had such fond memories of Bess.

Within four hours they were there, or as close as they could be. From the road according to their Sat Nav there was still one hundred and fifty metres of jungle to the clearing where Sam had trapped the Greenback monkeys. Rose and Harry left the Land Rover to investigate. Sam stayed with the animals; he was feeling too weak to come with them. There was a footpath which led all the way to the clearing, the ground was mostly firm and even. All they needed to do now was make the path wide enough to enable the Land Rover and trailer to get through. With the machetes they had brought with them they set about cutting a path through the jungle. It was hard and hot work; Harry was surprised how Rose coped so well, it took all his effort just to keep up with her. Sam was too weak to help, he stayed in the cage with the Greenbacks.

After several hours' work the path was clear and

wide enough for the Land Rover to get through. Harry reflected with Rose on how all those years ago Sam and his guide had had to cut through miles of jungle to reach the clearing. It had taken him so much effort just to create a one-hundred-and-fifty-metre path. Rose drove the Land Rover into the clearing, circled round to face the way it had come with the rear doors to the cage facing the clearing. Sam used as much strength as he had left and opened the doors and then climbed out into the clearing. He dropped to his knees and cried. The stress of the last few months had taken its toll on him. There he was, more than one hundred and twenty years later at the spot where it all started, not with Baccary this time but with Baccary's great-granddaughter and his great-grandson. After all this time, the end, the end of this great adventure was near. He turned and hugged Harry and Rose; they all cried some more. The monkeys stayed in the safety of the cage.

They had planned to stay the night as it was too far and too late to return home. Rose and Harry set up camp, they pitched their tents and made up a fire. Or it was more like Rose pitched the tents and made up a fire. Harry was ready and willing, but he was a spent force, the exertion of hacking through the jungle to widen the path had exhausted him, his skills he felt lay elsewhere. Gradually over the course of the evening the monkeys left the cage, the smallest one first then the other two. They stayed close to Sam. They stayed by Sam all night but by the morning they were gone. They had disappeared back into the jungle almost as swiftly as they had arrived years ago. Sam, Rose and Harry didn't try to find out where they had gone, they had gone, back to where they really belonged. Rose and Harry packed everything away; Sam was too weak to help. They knew they needed to get him home, back home to Tollesbury as soon as they could. Sam and Harry hadn't really thought about getting home, their plan ended with getting the Greenback monkeys back to their home. Rose, resourceful as ever, had thought about it and had booked them on a flight leaving Accra in two days.

They returned to Rose's home later that day. Sam was clearly very weak now the curse was lifting and he was aging fast. Harry spoke privately to Rose, to express his concerns about getting Sam back home in his weak state. Rose had thought of that too and had booked herself onto the flight with them. She reassured Harry that between them they would manage. Harry was relieved; it was what he had wanted but didn't want to ask. He didn't want to leave Rose, he wanted to stay, but he had to get Sam home. A day later they had landed at Heathrow and were in a hire car heading for Tollesbury.

Sam lived for three more days. He was cared for by the two people who loved him most, in the village that he loved. He was finally at peace; he could join his beloved Esme and family.

Sam Shine is buried in the graveyard at Tollesbury next to his wife Esme and alongside Charlotte, George, David and Emma.

Rose didn't return to Ghana for a long time. A lot of people from Ghana came to Tollesbury. They came to her wedding when she married Harry Wright. Six months, three weeks and two days after they had first met.

If you lived next door to Harry you would think he was just a normal man living a normal life and working in a normal job as a shipping agent. Yes, you might think of him as being reasonably well off and you certainly would not deny that he had the most beautiful wife. However, you would never, ever believe that he had the most extraordinary story to tell.

THE END

About the Author

Dan Walker is a retired school teacher based in Hertfordshire. He started his teaching career in 1975 and ended it 44 years later as the director of a London Teaching School having had a most rewarding, enjoyable and fun-filled career. His passion has always been for sailing. Since his teenage years he has owned and sailed boats on the River Blackwater in Essex.

He enjoys storytelling, whether that be in school assemblies, during lessons or on school journeys. He believes that the art of storytelling has long been overlooked and that listening to a good, well-told story is a joy.

Sam Shine and the Curse of the Greenback Monkeys is the first and one of his most popular stories which he has enjoyed telling for several years. It is followed by other adventures of Sam Shine, known as his missing years.

Printed in Great Britain
by Amazon